Tzu Kingdom

Paw in Paw

Karen Chilvers & Gill Eastgate

Illustrated by Michelle Smith

Published by New Generation Publishing in 2019

First Edition

ISBN 978-1-78955-627-8

www.newgeneration-publishing.com

New Generation Publishing

For Paddy and Mac

Tzu Kingdom supporters

Thank you to Santa Paws' Benevolent Fund

for your ongoing support

Lee Maddrey Fallon & Seamus

Sponsors of the Front Cover

The front cover illustration of young Coffee and young Bailey on the boat "Lady Latte of the Lake" is sponsored by Barb, Jeff and Cedar Reisler.

The drawing is inspired by the real-life story of Coffee and Bailey and features much of their own true stories.

Bailey's rescue, as written in 'Paw in Paw', is not dissimilar to his actual last-minute rescue and, yes, Coffee really does have a boat and the locations do exist on Lake Ontario, Canada.

We hope their love story inspires you.

"Coffee makes everything possible".

Sponsor of the Back Cover

The back cover illustration of Paddy and Stanley is sponsored by Mac with Alex and Damien Whittle.

The two little pals on a 'mission-possible' is the perfect sponsorship for their fun friend and fellow scout Mac.

Friends are always there for each other and as we discover in this adventure, Mac delivers friendship by the spoonful!

"Thank you for being our friend".

Name a Character Sponsors

Thank you to the following sponsors of characters who feature in Book 3.

Bryan Gallacher for **Brodie**

Andy Neufeld for **Rousey & Zeus**

Stephanie Watts Quam for **Otis**

Illustration Sponsors

The following sponsored images in Book 3:

- Abbi, Cassie &Lucy Bayliss sponsor 'Fitness Boys'
- Christine & Stella sponsor 'Costume Rescue'
- Claire, Freddie & Poppy sponsor 'Lennon'
- Debbie, Paddy and Mitch sponsor 'Sark'
- Linda & Louis sponsor 'Eiffel Tower'
- Susan Emery & Leon the Cat sponsor 'Cake'
- Heather, Finn & Luna Hays sponsor 'Renew'
- Yamilet Neufeld sponsors 'Sammy'
- Sharon & Millie Newman sponsor 'Puppies in Scout Tower'
- Wendy, Winny & Otto Simko sponsor 'Tzu Bakers'.

Friends of Tzu Kingdom

The following helped us to publish Book 3:

- Catherine Armstrong
- Diane Bayliss
- Christine & Stella Cannizzo
- Claire Chilvers
- Deneena & Beckham Davis
- Maureen Eastgate
- Susan Emery
- Lee Maddrey Fallon
- Ray Foreman
- Heather, Finn & Luna Hays
- Debbie Hoyt
- Carol Morrison & Brodie
- Debi Mullahy, Percy & Oliver
- Andrew Neufeld
- Sharon & Millie Newman
- Linda Price
- Barb & Jeff Reisler
- Debbie, Paddy & Mitch Robinson
- Santa Paws Shay
- Wendy, Winny & Otto Simko
- Maria Stevens

- Freddie Suett

- Karen Threadgold

- Stephanie Watts Quam

- Alex Whittle

- Alice, Amanda & Jeremy Williams

Also, thank you to Melanie & Molly Yeomans for the English to French translations and Wendy Simko for the original Tzu Kingdom Bus concept and adding the finishing touches to the front cover image.

Name a Character Sponsors

Thank you Catherine & Pixie Armstrong, Andrew & Sammy Neufeld, Maria Stevens and Stephanie Watts Quam & Bentley for sponsoring future characters **Kaos, Rascal, Opie** and **Zuzu**.

We will meet them all in Book 4...

Queen Coffee's Prologue

About six hundred dog years ago, Shih Tzus only lived in one land. It was in the Far, Far East and they had lived, played and cuddled there for thousands of dog years before that.

It was a beautiful summer day and they were so happy skipping, jumping and chasing each other about in their palace grounds.

All of a sudden, from absolutely nowhere, a freak storm began. The sun went into hiding and gave way to intense windy rain, black clouds, thunder and lightning.

It caught the tzus unaware and they ran for cover and waited for the storm to pass.

The storm stopped as suddenly as it had begun and the gang ventured out of their hiding place – the adult tzus first for safety, ushering the youngsters out when they knew it was safe.

Even though the sturdy tzus were unscathed by the storm, some more delicate creatures were not so fortunate.

As they gathered up their toys, one of the youngest tzus, Leo, heard a faint cry of help. It was coming from the lake. They had never ventured so far before, but now, someone clearly needed their help.

They ran down the grassy slopes as fast as their little legs could go and found fairies of all colours caught in an enormous fishing net, tired, upset and exhausted.

They too had been taken by surprise, blown off course by the winds and were now trapped with their intricate wings, and their very lives, in serious peril.

Without even thinking, Leo divided the tzus in to action teams and they all set to work with their nimble paws and delicate teeth, working in pairs to unhook every fairy and his or her tiny wings. The complicated rescue was eventually completed with all fairies free, unhurt and fluttering once again. It had taken hours, in to the night, but the tzus and their teamwork, patience and skill had saved the fairies from perishing.

Leo and his friends wished the fairies well and went back to the palace, pleased to be able to help and proud of how they had all worked together.

The next day, he was surprised to see a small delegation of fairies appear at the gates of their home. They thanked the tzus once again for saving them from such mortal danger and asked if there was anything they could gift to them. The tzus turned to Leo – after all it had been his long ears that had heard their cries for help.

Leo could only think of one thing after his adventure to the lake...to see the world.

The fairies then decreed that all Shih Tzus could use their fairy door network to visit new lands...shrinking down to squeeze through with fairy magic.

After this, Shih Tzus started to spread out through the world, making new friends and settling in new lands. Nonetheless they missed snuggling up, eating and playing games with each other and soon wished they had somewhere to meet up and this time, they asked the fairies for their help.

The fairies understood and set about setting up a palace within the fairy kingdom where the tzus could meet. They called it Tzu Kingdom on the condition that they would keep it beautiful, they would keep it secret and that they would elect the wisest tzu to be their King or Queen and they would see that it was always used for good.

The tzus accepted this offer and were quick to make Leo their first King for his bravery and leadership qualities.

Over the next few years, Leo made Tzu Kingdom what it is today and laid down the foundations for all future Kings and Queens to keep the promise they made to the fairies...

Chapter 1

Queen Coffee held Nancy tight as they soared over the clouds.

"Higher, higher," yelled Coffee, her long, silky ears fluttering in the wind as they flew.

"I thought you got dizzy at heights these days?" laughed her best friend and bridesmaid Nancy as the mountain range came in to view.

"Oh Nancy, you know me, I feel as safe in your paws as I do in Bailey's".

Nancy smiled. "That makes me happy," she said, "knowing that he keeps you safe and you two are so perfect together, possibly the best rulers Tzu Kingdom has ever had, looking after us all, paw in paw".

They giggled a little, knowing that the Kingdom was indeed in safe paws and everything was good.

"We're here...look..." said Nancy. Coffee gasped; she couldn't believe her beautiful brown eyes.

"Biscuit Mountain...it's more wonderful than I ever imagined".

Despite being a Canadian and used to mountains, this was the most gigantic one she had ever seen. Layers upon layers of biscuits were stacked before them with jam fillings, frosting and icing gleaming and sparkling in the sun.

They landed on a small shelf and breathed the aroma in deeply through their short snouts, the biscuit air made them tingle from nose to plume.

"Nancy have you been here before?" asked Coffee of her sweet friend.

"I came here for the very first time yesterday Miss Coffee my dear and I knew you would love it, so I just had to show you! I do love you sweetie; I am so glad you married Bailey and are so happy together...I am so proud of how you look after all the tzus and you know my Maisie and Beth love you to the moon don't you? Don't ever change..."

* * *

Coffee woke with a start – Momma was calling her in from the kitchen and it was time for breakfast. 'Oh, what a funny dream – 'Biscuit Mountain'!' She remembered it all so clearly and decided that she would pop through to Tzu Kingdom later and tell her husband Bailey. Oh, how he would love the idea of a mountain made of jammy biscuits!

Chapter 2

Stifling a little burp as she jumped through the fairy door, Coffee saw Lennon on the Welcome Room desk, playing a soft and gentle tune on his acoustic guitar.

"Woo hoo Lennon just popping in quickly to see King Bailey is he here do you know?" she cheerfully waved, a song in her voice.

"Yes, my Queen but..."

"Can't stop just now Lennon, Momma is taking me out to get groceries at market, but I had to tell him about the most glorious dream I had..."

She scampered down the corridors to the Royal Quarters from where Bailey and she ruled Tzu Kingdom with love, fairness and bravery. Straight into the room she burst, laughing....

"Bailey, Bailey I had the funniest dream..."

She wasn't prepared for what she saw. Snuggled in to a beanbag was Bailey, with tiny Maisie, Nancy's sister, crying in to his fur.

"Oh, my darling Coffee," said Bailey, jumping up with Maisie in his paws, still sniffling, "Maisie bravely came through to tell us some sad news...our dear friend Nancy has passed away in her sleep".

Coffee stumbled and fell in to his fur, sobbing.

"She is with her human Dad Ifan now, you know how she missed him this past couple of weeks and now they are reunited, beyond the clouds with her mother too. She had a wonderful life and you were a big part of it and, oh, I expect she has met up with dear Wolfgang".

3

Bailey continued but Coffee was in a tizzy, her head spinning and hardly able to catch her breath.

Nancy was one of the oldest tzus in the Kingdom and she had never really known it without her.

Bailey and Maisie held her tight as she thought of their friendship, the fun they had, and her mind went back further and further until it landed way back in time...

Chapter 3

SEVEN YEARS EARLIER...

"Morning Coffee my sweet – early to start your shift as always,"
chirped Chief Scout Nancy as her protégé jumped off the Scout
Tower rope ladder in her crisp uniform - landing expertly - and
saluted her with a smile and a twinkle in her eye.

"Well there's tzus to be rescued, fairy doors to be catalogued
and 'Meet and Greets' to be arranged. I left Momma dozing
on the porch with her book and Dad mowing the grass! It's
going to look lovely this Summer with all our new flowers
and... we have lodgers for the Spring!"

"Really?" Nancy gasped, turning away from the telescope for
a minute, "who?"

Coffee giggled.

"A little family of robins have moved in to our barn. They are
so sweet. Momma and I are leaving mealworms and seeds
out for them. Oh, I do hope they'll be happy at my house, we
have done all we can to make them welcome".

Nancy felt a glow of love for her best friend, she was ever so
special. Friendly, warm, caring, loving - no one had a bad
word to say about her and she was such a hoot at any social
occasion.

She hoped the robins would thank Coffee when they flew the
nest or she would feel quite upset, just like last year.

"I'm sure they will be the best looked after robins in the
world".

Nancy briefed Coffee on the latest Scout Tower news. They had identified some new tzus to join the party on Friday and the young fur made notes. She had taken responsibility for installing fairy doors and meeting any tzus that had recently reached two in human years and, therefore, were of the right age to join the fun in Tzu Kingdom.

"Well I have a busy day! After I check the fairy door numbers, I shall pop to New Jersey later today and extend a paw to Lola and then chop chop, straight to the Lake District to meet Kiki, quick as a bunny, I'll run off to find Colin in London. Then I shall bring my notes back and check all is well and home...phew!"

Nancy smiled as Coffee skipped to the kitchen to get some fruit juice, singing as she went. One day soon, Nancy was going to have to retire from her position as Chief Scout and she looked to Coffee as her successor.

Young Miss Coffee was destined for great things.

"Coffee dear, are you OK to hold the fort for a while? I have my fortnightly meeting with King Pierre shortly. Everyone is working away quietly today, so I don't think there's anything to worry about".

"Of course, Chief Scout Nancy," she hollered from the kitchen, "I'll just get a power juice and a Tzu Bakery cupcake for each of the team and let them have a quick break and then they will be all refreshed and happy to work. Please tell our dear King Pierre that all is well here in Scout Tower".

Nancy descended the tower on the rope ladder, rather carefully. She was fourteen in human years now, but her skill and practice made it easy. She loved being Chief Scout and she had good reason to remain in the tower but events at home had meant that she had to take some difficult decisions and today was the day to talk to her King and good friend.

Nancy had known two rulers before Pierre: King Hamish for a brief while when she first arrived in Tzu Kingdom and then Mirabelle, the young Queen who she became close friends with to the point where she became her trusted advisor and key courtier.

Mirabelle entrusted Nancy with the secret of Tzu Kingdom, passed down from the third ruler, Queen Sally. The secret was held in a book that was sealed in the wall of the Comforter Kitchen but that must not be touched until the time was right and that would be when the Kingdom burped it up from the waters.

It made no sense to Nancy, but she had a job that Mirabelle had given her. She was to watch for a Canadian beauty with long flowing ears and cappuccino eyes and a wise, kind-eyed Tzu from England with a Sirius star and ensure they fell in love. For they were the chosen ones upon whom Tzu Kingdom depended.

And, so she had, and when Pierre became King in 2004, seven years ago she passed the secret she kept to him. They waited and looked. They looked and waited. Nancy became Chief Scout and looked some more.

After four years, they had begun to think it was just a myth until the day that Nancy went to meet and greet a shih tzu called Coffee in a Toronto park.

She watched from a fairy door as she ran down the hill with her Momma and Dad, laughing and skipping. She admired her beauty but it all fell in to place when she stopped, and her ears swung back and forth as she waited for her parents to catch up.

A shiver went down Nancy's spine as she got her first sight of one of the chosen ones. Coffee. With the cappuccino eyes.

But the wait for the second one was to go on for a few more years yet.

Chapter 4

"Oh Pierre, Pierre, Pierre," laughed Nancy as she took her tea and biscuit from him in the Royal Chamber, "when will he ever arrive, and will we live to see it?" she chortled.

King Pierre set his cup and saucer down and twiddled with his moustache.

"I hope so, I so want to meet him, and we know it must be soon because, there is no doubt that Coffee is one of the chosen ones. But we must think practically, who knows when they will fall in love? Plus, neither of us is a pup. I think we should look to the future and share the secret with some more trusted tzus".

He paused and thought deeply. He had been looking for a time to tell Nancy he had some exciting news, and this seemed like a good time. His Maman and Papa were soon to adopt a brother and sister who were to be called Franc and Centime. In time, he would bring them through to Tzu Kingdom and he had decided that it would be perfect if they were to take up positions in the Comforter Wing where any rescues would be taken and nursed back to health. He thought that they should be trained by Comforters Mabel and Myrtle and that they would then be told about the secret book, sealed in the wall until the time was right.

Nancy agreed with his suggestion, to be a comforter was a privilege and it was ideal for the King's siblings. She wanted to talk to him about something too. Recently, her human mother had passed away and she felt that she needed to spend more time with Ifan, her dad. Especially now her human sister Megan was married and living abroad with one small daughter named Fleur and another baby on the way. It was just the two of them in their bungalow and he needed looking after. So, although she would certainly continue to keep watch over

Coffee until her counterpart was found, she didn't feel she could look after Scout Tower too. Something had to give.

Pierre nodded. He had noticed she was weary and had a solution, just like always.

"I think it is time to promote young Miss Coffee. We should make her Chief Scout. She will be excellent – you always feel more than happy leaving her in charge and she always rises to the occasion - and you can train her over the next couple of months. I know her first reaction will be that she couldn't possibly be so senior...but we know she can!"

Nancy agreed, happily and they said they would meet with her in the next few days and talk her in to it.

"It's so hard keeping an eye on her now – all the boys want to dance with her and I have to keep shooing young Lennon and young Tanner away! Plus, every time she goes to the Comforter Wing Rousey and Brodie blush...I think it's those ears!"

"Well," agreed the King of Tzus, "even the new young Santa Paws, Seamus, had his head turned when he visited me last month. He quite lost his train of thought for a few minutes, I had to change the subject to more serious matters to keep his mind of our Miss Coffee!"

"Oh Pierre, I am exhausted with it all – she needs a dance partner. I am far too old for energetic cha cha chas!!!"

They laughed and finished their teas.

***

Up in Scout Tower, a pair of cappuccino eyes were looking through a telescope. Their owner gasped. She had caught site of a tzu in need of a rescue. She peered at the abandoned dog and, although matted and dirty, she could see he had a perfect Sirius marking on top of his head.

As she zoned in on him, he turned and a pair of kind, wise eyes met hers for a second. She gasped, and her paw went to her mouth, butterflies swirled in her stomach and she felt hot and out of breath.

"Oh goodness," said Coffee, having never felt that way before and not quite sure what it was.

She shook her fur, fanned herself with her paw and made a note that there was a lost tzu in peril that needed to be found.

She looked back through the scope, but she couldn't see any trace of him. Sighing, Coffee sipped her juice.

'I will find that darling tzu,' she thought, moving to the Special Ops telescope with a mission.

Chapter 5

Checking his booking confirmation once more, Scout Winny hurried down the river path to where he would meet his new friend Bentz to learn a new skill. He could barely wait!

He had waited until his Mommy went to work and then, with his brother Otto, jumped through their fairy door to the Welcome Room. Otto was off for his regular shift at the Comforter Wing where he had recently been appointed to the team, looking after rescued tzus. They burped loudly, hugged and headed off to start their days but today, Winny wasn't heading to Scout Tower, he was off to be trained at one of the oldest institutions in Tzu Kingdom – Tzu Bakery.

He had tasted the doughnuts, cakes and bread but today, he would be part of it and it would his new hobby. He had tried a little knitting but it wasn't his thing so when he saw a leaflet in the café offering a short course, he jumped at the chance and, asking his new friend Bentz made it even more exciting.

Winny's eyes lit up when the gleaming white building came in to view as he walked closer to the river. He saw the pedal bikes with baskets and trailers that were used to deliver the baked treats around the Kingdom and the barge on the river that took large orders to other dog worlds.

He pushed open the door to the lounge with excitement and anticipation. It was packed out! Most of the metal and jewel pups were there and, in the corner with his sisters Michelle, Rosa, Ellen and Molly, was Bentz and he went over to say hello.

The kitchen was still hidden behind a bi-folding shutter and some drinks, cookies and mini cheese scones had been laid out on the tables.

Molly spied him first and nudged Bentz, who had his back to the entrance.

"WINNY PAL!" he exclaimed as he ran to embrace him. They had begun to strike up a special bond since Bentz had settled with his new human family in Seattle, "Let me introduce you to my sisters and some of the metal and jewel pups...we all did a mission together a while ago..."

Now Winny felt a little left out, like he was an outsider, "oh who did you rescue?" he asked, bravely, masking his worries.

"Oh," said Ellen, "there was a doggy in a bad home and she was put in a rescue centre and we had to go through and make this lady find and adopt her...it was funny! We had to dance in her garden – there were 18 of us plus rescuer Phoebe who was in charge!"

"It all worked out," continued Rosa, "the nice lady adopted her and she's called Luna now, she's the lead singer of Tzu Aroo, the Kingdom band..."

"What?" Winny couldn't believe it and this news made him feel so much happier, "my brother Otto and I used work for Luna as her minders before she was rehomed!"

Michelle smiled. "Well, look we all have things in common straight away!" Winny smiled back as they shared the scones and cookies.

The side door to the bakery kitchen opened and there was a professional baker, Jiro, Acting Chief Baker.

"Good morning all!" Jiro shouted, cheerily.

"Good morning Chief Baker," they bellowed back, in unison.

"Lovely to see you all, so let's get this day started! I would like you to get yourselves into pairs, go over to the laundry store, put on a chef jacket, write your name on a chef hat, pop that on and, if you have long ears please clip them up with the fur clips you will find on the table. Finally come through here to wash your paws and assemble at a workstation with another pair".

The excitement was building as a paw stampede made its way to the laundry store.

Chapter 6

"Can we share your workstation?" asked Michelle and Molly as they clipped up each other's ears.

"We would be delighted!" said Winny, mesmerised by Michelle's glowing black locks and Molly's curly white fur.

He did up his jacket and put his hat on. His ears were shorter than the girls and they fitted neatly under his hat.

"Erm, excuse me, erm, Winny, erm help..." came a voice from the floor. He looked down, there was Bentz knotted up in a jacket, writhing around in a peculiar tangle.

Winny gasped then giggled. His back paws were in the jacket front, and that was upside down, and inside out. His hat was tangled in a sleeve and he rushed to help.

"Oh Bentz, this is a predicament and no mistake! Here, let me help you..." he said as he untangled his friend. In a few seconds he was free and stood up, a little embarrassed.

"Let's try this again," Winny said, holding out the jacket the right way around for Bentz to put his paws in. He buttoned him up and spun him around, he looked very smart.

"Thanks Winny, it's not like my café apron, that's easy to put on. Can I do anything to help you?"

He couldn't really, he had it all under control but Bentz so wanted to help him so he thought really hard until...

"Oh yes, you could write our names on our hats!"

"Yes, I can do that!" he picked up a colourful pen and wrote their names on a hat each, proudly presenting it to his pal.

Winny, didn't know what to say, it was written so beautifully but there was something wrong.

"Erm, my name it has two Ns in but it doesn't matter, it fine like this..."

"I can fix it don't you worry!" Bentz took his glitter pen and drew a little arrow up between the I and the N and added the extra N. "There".

Winny loved it. It would always be one of his most treasured possessions. He popped it on his head, tucking his own ears in, picked a blue clip out and helped Bentz clip his long ears up under his hat.

They were ready for their baking challenge and went in to join the class.

Chapter 7

In they scurried, looking for Michelle and Molly. The girls jumped and waved from the front. Bentz rolled his eyes jokingly at his pal, he knew they would be at the front! It was quite dark, but they made it to their workstation where they could make out three tzu shapes in the shadows, standing in a row.

"Lights please," said Jiro firmly and clapped his paws together twice. From behind the three bakers bright strip lighting illuminated the bakery and it travelled in a domino effect across the ceiling until the whole place was lit and they could see how bright, clean and shiny it was.

Every tzu gasped as they took in the sights and smells of Tzu Bakery. The marble counter tops gleamed and from them arose the aroma of fresh lemon that tickled their short snuffly noses as they breathed it in, on each counter was a sparkling mixer, all around them hanging from ceiling hooks were pots and pans, piled neatly along one wall was a sea of cake tins, cupcake trays and brass moulds. A dresser at the back was chock full of stacks of both modern and antique crockery on which to serve the baked treats in the lounge and in a huge cloth-lined wicker basket were rolling pins ready for making perfect pastry.

Behind their tutors were cupboards full of ingredients: canisters lined up with every type of flour from cake flour to bread flour and almond flour to potato flour. The sugars – from turbinado to sanding sugar and from muscovado to Baker's Special Sugar.

Inquisitively, Molly raised her paw. "Excuse me Acting Chief Baker Jiro, where does that sparkly door behind you lead to?" she asked, transfixed by a glistering door that seemed to change colour as she stared.

Jiro and his team laughed.

"That's the sprinkle cupboard Molly. It has potent magic properties and, well, we must keep it under lock and key. You see, we make the magic sprinkles for Santa Paws here and export to him or her when it's almost ready. Things happen when you eat sprinkles, maybe have a word with Deputy Chief Scout Stanley?"

The class looked at each other confused, they wanted to try the sprinkles now even if they hadn't before and they were certainly going to ask Stanley when they next saw him.

"Now, time for introductions," Jiro said, bringing the class to order, "to my left is Freda and to my right is Greta, twin sisters and my most senior bakers".

They stepped forward on their left paw and curtsied, completely in tandem, transfixing everyone. You couldn't tell them apart and Bentz looked at his own sisters, all four so different – Michelle glossy black, Molly sparkling white and Rosa and Ellen both multi-coloured and he was blond. Yes, they were similar in how they looked and acted but twins? This was a phenomenon.

"Today, we are going to take you through some basic recipes. You will learn to make and sculpt bread, bake sausage rolls, pipe pastry 'pawmiers' and then you will, in your pairs, bake and ice your own, customised, cupcakes, all Tzu Bakery classics. You can take some to enjoy in the lounge after our lesson and, also, we will share them throughout the kingdom, as is the tzu ethos".

Everyone nodded, that seemed like an excellent idea.

Chapter 8

The bakers were impressed with their students.

"That's it team, put your paws in to that kneading, add the yeast when Freda or Greta give you the nod and get ready to shape it in to whatever you chose...footballs, fairy doors, self-pawtraits...you choose," Jiro instructed. The class was impressive and his deputies walked around the room in tandem, admiring the pawdiwork.

"Good paw work..."

"Bentz...super kneading..."

"Winny..." said Freda and Greta.

The boys couldn't tell them apart so just addressed them both as "Miss" to save their blushes. They were transfixing, they spoke whole sentences together, with one finishing off what the other started.

"Have you given..."

"...any thought to what..."

"...you are going to sculpt..."

"...your bread in to?" continued the twin bakers.

"Frogs!" said Winny and Bentz together, laughing as they had just discovered they both loved frogs and had made plans to go to the pond and do some frog watching one day soon.

"You don't want..."

"...to each do..."

"...something..."

"...different?" they asked.

Bentz and Winny looked at them incredulously.

"Well, no of course not," Bentz piped up, "frogs like to be together with their friends".

The twins laughed, they understood.

"Girls what will ..."

"...you be sculpting?"

Molly looked up from her workstation to reveal her floral bread project. "Do you like it, it's 'une jolie fleur de pain'? Mummy makes them at home, you can break off petals to share with friends".

"It's quite..."

"...stunning..." they agreed.

Michelle was working diligently on hers. It was intricate, and she was concentrating hard until, finally, she stood back.

"There, one 'Statue of Liberty Bread Masterpiece'!"

It certainly was and the tzus were so excited as they took their individual masterpieces to the proving oven, where their bread would rise before baking. They admired each other's work before they returned to make sausage rolls.

* * *

Time marched on and class was amazing fun. Trays of sausage rolls were baked and they smelt divine. Jiro had let them all have a couple for lunch and the rest were packed away for taking home and sharing.

After lunch, Pawmiers had been crafted from all butter puff pastry and cinnamon. It was such fun rolling the pastry in to

19

make paw-shaped spirals. They chilled it, like Jiro showed them on his own workstation, sliced with a flour dusted safety knife and baked them for 15 minutes in the pastry ovens.

"These just melt in your mouth," Michelle exclaimed.

Chapter 9

Standing back to admire their pawdiwork, Winny and Bentz couldn't be prouder.

After the final break of the day, with the memories of strawberry milkshakes still in their heads, they had listened whilst Jiro presenting the final challenge of the day. Cupcakes.

The cakes had been baked and, as a treat for being such good students, they were to ice them in whatever colours they chose. They were also able to take dishes of any toppings they liked – jelly tots, smarties, mini biscuits, wafer curls and, from the locked cupboard, magic sprinkles.

Jiro knew his trade, he had explained that the best colours for rainbow cupcakes were yellow, blue and pink squished in an icing bag together. As soon as they heard the words, Bentz and Winny wanted to do nothing but!

They took dishes of the three colours and carefully placed enormous dollops of tasty buttercream icing in the bags, squished and then started to pipe.

They swirled the icing into little mountains and decorated them with tiny biscuits. They piped little stars and decorated them with glistering sprinkles so it looked like the starry sky above and enormous twirled flowers with smarties.

When Greta and Freda arrived, they were impressed too.

In their pairs, the class laid their cupcakes out on to the pretty antique china plates in the centre of their tables, placing them alongside their sausage rolls, pawmiers and bread masterpieces.

Their tutors moved to the other end of the room by the shutter.

"Well class, I am immensely proud. You have been exemplary today and just look at these showstopping cupcakes now! If you would just all stand by your workstations in your fours as we welcome our special guest quality controllers..."

The twin sisters pushed the shutter to the lounge open with an enormous clutter noise to reveal, none other than King Bailey and Queen Coffee.

Everyone gasped at the most special of guests and Winny turned to Bentz, but he wasn't there.

* * *

Winny spun all the way round, he had right next to him a moment before and he couldn't have moved that fast. He felt a tug on his chef jacket. Bentz was under the desk, shaking.

"Bentz, what's the matter? It's our King and Queen, you aren't scared, are you? You love them dearly right, like we all do?"

He nodded, tears in his big eyes. "It's the noisy shutter, I don't like it, it reminds me of before...bad stuff..."

Cradling his pal in his paws he let his tears roll on to his fur. Bentz had been through a traumatic time before he came to Tzu Kingdom. He stroked his friend's fur.

"Bentz, you have me now and I am going to keep you safe for always OK? Whenever you feel sad or scared, you look for your best friend Winny OK? If I am not with you, then close your eyes and see my face, and know that I love you to the moon, right? Now, hold my paw, stand up brave as a lion right by my side and let's show the chosen ones our brilliant baked stuff!"

Chapter 10

King Bailey and Queen Coffee passed each table admiring what had been baked.

"Pawmiers! I love these," said Bailey, sampling a delicious pastry treat from every workstation as he walked to the front.

The pups were so pleased with themselves as they stopped for a chat with each group of students, thanking them for taking the time to learn a new skill.

They reached the front and admired the rainbow cupcakes.

"Jiro, Freda, Greta, you have managed another wonderful training day here, would it be appropriate for King Bailey and I to say a few words?" she asked, turning to her husband.

But Bailey was busy 'sampling' and quite forgetting himself. He looked up at her, mouth full of pawmiers, startled.

"Well, maybe it's best if I say a few words today?" said Coffee, to everyone's amusement. Bailey nodded, quietly munching on his pastries.

"Furs," said the Queen, "I was simply going to thank you all for making all these wonderful treats and I hope some of you go on to be bakers here in Tzu Bakery. You may not be aware but, King Bailey himself was a baker before he became our King and doughnuts were his speciality, although he has a taste for pastry as we can see," she giggled, "so, I am sure Jiro will be happy to see some of you here as an occasional Tzu Baker".

"But most of all, I want to thank you for upholding the traditions of Tzu Kingdom and now, I think, it is time for us all to retire to the lounge with a plateful of yum!"

* * *

They relaxed in the lounge, with a happy Bentz sitting with Queen Coffee whilst she straightened his top knot.

Winny smiled as he brought over some more cupcakes. Today had been a brilliant day and now, he had to have a little best friend chat because he was on a mission.

Chapter 11

Stanley was in Mama's office. He had been snoozing in his basket by her desk but now he was awake. Mama was having a sob and he paw patted at her knees to see if she was alright and let her know he was here for her, always.

She lifted him up and held him in her arms.

"Oh Stanners my darling, I just read a wee story about shih tzu love and it made me all emotional".

He looked in to her eyes, inquisitively. He loved Mama so much and he never liked to see her cry.

"There's this lovely lady with two little girls and, well, this is the sad bit, her husband died in mysterious circumstances on a business trip and she got quite a pay-out from his employers. She bought a big house in Wales and converted it so her father and his shih tzu could live next door in their own little annexe. Another sad bit, her father died a few months ago and so did his little dog, but they were both elderly..."

Stanley was wondering when the lovely bit would start, it was making him quite forlorn just now.

Mama picked up the story again.

"Anyway, so now the annexe is vacant they are going to use it as a sanctuary for tzus-less-fortunate! Finding homes for the little ones with no one to love them, helping those that are troubled and need rehabilitation and providing a forever home for those that are ill and can't be rehomed. They will all enjoy happiness and comfort at Nancy Noodle House!"

"What's even more wonderful is that Megan has two shih tzus of her own now too – they both just turned up in her garden and stayed forever!"

Stanley's ears pricked up. Something was starting to sound terribly familiar about this story.

"Want to play 'swings and roundabouts?'" Mama asked.

"Wheeeeeeeeeee..." she squealed as they swung around on the office chair..."wheeeeeeeee"..."once more... wheeeeee" Stanley laughed and barked. He loved their special 'mother and son' time in the office. This was their little secret, not even Dad knew that they played this game! They had been playing it ever since he was a little puppy and he first started working in Mama's tailoring empire. He loved his job here at home, as much as he loved being Deputy Chief Scout of Tzu Kingdom as Chief Scout Paddy's second-in-command.

Mama squeezed him tight and kissed his tummy. She stood up with him in her arms and then popped him down in her chair.

"Wait here darling, I am just going to make a cup of coffee and get the phone charger," she said as she ventured downstairs.

Stanley turned to the computer and reached out for her spare reading glasses, balancing them on his short snout with precision. The story Mama read was still on screen and he leaned in to read it.

His eyes were drawn to the picture and he couldn't believe what he saw in front of him – he knew it had sounded familiar. Sat in a garden he knew very well was Maisie, his girlfriend, her little sister Beth and their enchanted human sisters Skye and Fleur, all smiling and surrounding their Mummy Megan on a wrought iron bench.

He was so excited! They were looking for two members of staff to live in to permanently care for the dogs that were there. It was going to be paradise if Maisie's house was anything to judge it by!

"You know Stan, if we win the lottery, we should buy some land and do something similar. We could build an annexe for Granny too..." shouted Mama as she climbed the stairs.

Stanley loved that idea! Imagine if Granny lived next door! Mama was nearly back in the office so he quickly removed her spectacles from his nose and placed them back on the desk where he found them. Mama couldn't suspect a thing, not least that he could read and write, so he snuggled down on the chair, pretending to have been asleep.

He wouldn't say anything to Maisie just yet, she was no doubt preparing to surprise him and he smiled at thoughts of his beloved organising the unveiling of Nancy Noodle House, named after her much-missed older sister, former Chief Scout and Queen Coffee's closest friend.

Chapter 12

Nancy's memorial service was full of laughter and cheer, just as she would have wanted and, in fact, clearly instructed the ever-pragmatic Beth, her smallest sister.

Nancy had lived over 20 human years – over 100 in dog years - and she wanted her friends to be grateful for having known her and enjoying her life with her, not sad that she had crossed over the rainbow bridge. It was her time.

Queen Coffee was so brave as she regaled the tales of their younger days when they danced the Furry Tail Fandango and the Cha Cha Cha at parties. She told an incredible tale of a rescue of two puppies from a motorway service station where they were being passed from bad humans to bad humans and whilst they were arguing about money they raced around the cars, grabbed a puppy each and jumped through the fairy door, running up to Scout Tower straight away with the pair still in their paws and watching the humans hunt, in vain, for hours, calling all the other scouts and even King Pierre himself, up to watch through the telescopes. The puppies, later named Cherry and Mimosa, laughed from the middle of the congregation as they too recalled their first visit to Tzu Kingdom.

King Bailey spoke of the wonderful job Nancy had made of looking after King Wolfgang recently and how they must be having a great time beyond the clouds together, knitting and drinking soup. He paid tribute to her service to the Kingdom, keeping the secret until the time was right to reveal it and for her dedication to King Pierre. She had always been so close to royalty and, yet, her paws had always been grounded.

Maisie and Beth recited a poem they had written about their big sister, holding paws on stage, showing the courage of lions, and making everyone laugh about Nancy's funny little ways. They ended by talking about the times they had had recently in their garden, when she dozed with Ifan whilst they played with Fleur and Skye, their human sisters.

Finally, Luna and Tzu Aroo started to play a gentle song, a favourite of Nancy's and everyone joined in.

Somewhere over the rainbow bridge up high
There's a land that I heard of once in a lullaby
Somewhere over the rainbow, skies are blue
And the dreams that you dare to dream really do come true

Someday I'll wish on Sirius star
And wake up where the clouds are far
Behind me
Where troubles melt like gravy drops
Away above the chimney tops
That's where you'll find me

Somewhere over the rainbow shih tzus fly
Tzus fly over the rainbow.
Why then, oh, why can't I?

If happy little tzu dogs fly
Beyond the rainbow.
Why, oh, why can't I?

Backstage, King Bailey scooped the girls up in his paws.

"Well done Beth and Maisie, you were ever so brave then, ever so brave. I feel that Nancy was maybe one of the happiest, most accomplished and most loved tzus in the world".

Maisie and Beth looked at each other, both raising an eyebrow.

"What?" Queen Coffee enquired.

29

"Well," Maisie began, jumping down and pacing, looking a little uncomfortable, "there was one thing that Nancy was quite sad about and she was going to talk to you both".

Beth jumped down and also began pacing around them. Coffee and Bailey's eyes followed as they circled around in front of them, as Luna sang sweetly on stage.

"You see, Nancy may have been delighted to be your bridesmaid when you eloped to Paris but she always felt sad that you didn't marry here in Tzu Kingdom..."

"...with all your friends..." Maisie continued, padding in a circle, "so we were thinking, in Nancy's honour..."

"...maybe you could renew your vows, here in Tzu Kingdom..."

"...and we could have a massive party!"

Stanley appeared, having snuck up the side stairs to join Maisie and congratulate the girls on their poem.

"A party? Yes please!" he said, excitedly, "what we celebrating?"

"Queen Coffee and King Bailey are going to get married again!" Beth squealed.

The Royal couple looked at each other and smiled.

"What do you think Sweetpea?" Bailey asked his wife.

It had been over three years since their wedding in Paris and their only guests that night had been Franc, Centime and Nancy, with the wedding conducted at Hotel Battenberg, the world's best dog hotel, officiated by Louis Battenberg, Canine Concierge and long-time friend of Bailey.

"Well, I don't know," she replied, stifling a giggle, "I mean it's your turn to propose, I asked you last time".

"Well you had turned me down twice," he laughed.

The young tzus looked at each other, this was news to them all and they didn't know what to say. They held their breath, not daring to interfere.

Then suddenly, Bailey got down on one furry knee and took Coffee's paws in his.

"My darling Coffee Cup, I love you to the moon and back and I ask you, please would you renew your vows to me and marry me again?"

"YES! YES! YES!" said the Queen as she dropped to her knees and hugged him.

"Third time lucky!" he winked to their young friends.

Chapter 13

Maisie, Stanley and Beth arrived at the café to find it packed out after the memorial.

Winny ran to greet them at the entrance. "Hello, hello, we are over here waiting for you...we couldn't sit in Bentz' section because we don't want him to overhear, right?"

He took Beth's paw and ran her on ahead. Maisie and Stanley running behind trying to keep up as Paddy came in to view, eating a doughnut covered in icing. He waved hello as he munched away.

"Help yourselves," he spluttered, "pushing the doughnut plate in to the middle of the table. They all picked a doughnut as the waiter delivered coffees and juices for the friends to have together and Maisie passed out some paw wipes. This was an official meeting of the team that Paddy had pulled together to find the long-lost mother of their friend Bentz and she didn't want sticky paws all over the papers, thank you very much.

"Well," said Stanley as he wiped his paws and mouth, "thank you for coming to the second of our meetings to find Bentz' mother. As agreed at the last meeting, from now on we will refer to this group as the 'Lemonade Mission', our project code word".

Stanley was heading up this project and he knew he had a great team around him. Beth was convinced that Bentz' mother was alive and had been rescued and, as the evidence was presented, he was pretty sure too.

"Shall we have a little recap then Winny and Beth?"

"Well," said Beth, pulling out a copy of a magazine from her satchel, "you will all be familiar with this magazine 'WOOF!' that gets delivered to many of our houses in the UK. A few weeks ago, Mummy Megan was reading something from here with Fleur about a young tzu that had been found in a ditch in a forest. She was discovered, exhausted and on the point of giving up, by a large dog called Maggie, a bearded collie, who barked and barked until her owners came over.

"Mummy said that they had taken her to their vets and got her checked over. So poorly, she spent three nights there on a drip but then, she recovered. Clearly, she had something to live for. Maybe, she knows Bentz is looking for her?"

"Well, they weren't able to take her in themselves, so they took her to a big rescue centre where they promised to care for her and find her new humans. It was in the Kent countryside, in England".

Everyone nodded. But Paddy had a question.

"Beth, how could you possibly know this is Bentz' mother?"

"Well, at this stage it was just a hunch. So, I shared it with Maisie".

Maisie picked up the story.

"That's right, we had to get our paws on that copy of 'WOOF!'. So, the next day we waited until Mummy Megan took Fleur and Skye to school. Beth kept watch from the back of the sofa and I jumped up on the armchair, took a daring leap across to the coffee table and landed on a pile of magazines. One by one, I pushed them on to the floor and then Beth and I flipped through the pages as fast as we could".

Beth flicked through the copy of 'WOOF!' on the table. She opened it on the big rescue story of the month and held it up for all to see.

She pointed to a cheery photo of a smiling lad in a wheelchair holding a stunning, long-haired silver shih tzu in his arms.

"Look close," said Beth, "where have you seen those eyes before?"

"BENTZ!" Paddy and Stanley gasped.

Chapter 14

"Those are Bentz' eyes indeed," Winny interjected, "but we had to get more information, so I hatched a plan to get some more information from Bentz without raising his suspicions".

Paddy and Stanley looked over with interest and a raised eyebrow each.

"I popped in a couple of weeks ago and sat in his section. I needed to spark up a conversation with him and I think fate played a part. There, on the table, was some information about a course at the Tzu Bakery. 'Hmmmm' I thought, I would love to know how to make cupcakes and, I mused to myself, I bet Bentz would too. So, when he came over with my banana milkshake, I just went right out and asked him. Brave as a lion".

"He agreed straight away, he wanted to go but not on his own and he said he would love to go with me. I hadn't really spoken to him much before that but, you know, as we started talking and laughing, I just thought, I think we are going to be really good friends".

Best friends Paddy and Stanley looked at each other. They had thought exactly the same the first time they had met too.

"Tzu Bakery was fun!" Winny continued. "We made rainbow cupcakes with icing and we added glittery sprinkles and jelly tots but, the most important thing is that we were able to talk about how we came to discover Tzu Kingdom and met all our friends and he told me about what happened to his mother. As he spoke, I made a few notes in my head and it seems that his mother was abandoned somewhere in Kent as the bad humans took him to the harbour where he was rescued – what we know as 'Wolfgang Waters'. That means that it all fits and there is every chance that we have found his mother".

There was a slight pause and they all looked at Stanley and Paddy, who seemed to be pondering something.

"...and the cupcakes?" Paddy enquired.

Winny laughed. "We put them in Tupperware behind the counter here to share. They just need defrosting!"

Stanley sniggered and brought the meeting back to order from the giggles that had begun.

"This all seems quite straightforward then. Surely, we just need to scan all the gardens in Kent and look for a Tzu that's not yet known to us. I mean, if we get a team on this and put the word out, we should get her found fairly soon".

"If only it were that simple," said Beth, flicking to the end of the article in the magazine.

- *Charlie's health and wellbeing improves every day with Elle by his side constantly. The family have recently begun a new life on an island in the sun where it is hoped that his health will continue to improve and only agreed to this interview for a donation to the charity that trained Elle to be a 'companion dog for a disabled child'. WOOF! wishes them well in their new home.*

The Lemonade Mission team looked deflated. The trail had gone cold and they knew not how to proceed.

"Hang on a tail-wagging second!" blurted out Maisie, suddenly.

"There's going to be a record somewhere and probably in the rescue where Elle was taken by Maggie and her kind family. Well, all we need to do is break in to the rescue and get hold of that record and we can find out where she is. They would have done a home check on the new place you would think, and we will have the address or something once we get those records".

36

Paddy shook his head and huffed, "all we have to do is break in, eh?"

Maisie nodded, placing her entire faith in Paddy. He would find a way. He was Chief Scout. He knew who to go to for advice and everything. She smiled, excitedly and melted his heart a little. Stanley's too. He picked up the magazine and read through the whole article, sipping his milkshake.

"Paddy, that's not as crazy as it sounds. Look, the rescue she went to – Battersea Brands Hatch – we know so many tzus that were rehomed from there – Lennon for a start - we must be able to work out how we can get in unnoticed, read Elle's records and discover her whereabouts".

Paddy leaned over and perused the article himself as Stanley pointed at the relevant paragraph.

"You're right. We can do this. Looks like we have a covert mission to plan," he smiled.

"YES!" hollered Maisie, Beth and Winny as they high pawed Paddy and Stan.

"I think we need those cupcakes now," Stanley said, seriously.

Chapter 15

As the Lemonade Team finished their cupcakes and threw around a few ideas about breaking in to the rescue centre, they were disturbed by Bentz himself.

Hurriedly, they tidied away their papers and notebooks, they didn't want to raise his hopes, so this had to be kept secret.

As they looked up, they noticed that everyone was heading to the Party Room.

"Royal Announcement!" gasped Bentz and started speed walking in to the next room, followed by his friends.

On the way Phoebe caught up with Paddy and he reached up to give her a kiss.

Kiki and Lola, Alice and Pom Pom were already in the room with Mac and Colin.

"What's going on?" said Mac, with worried ears.

"Oh, I think I might know," said Stanley, looking to Maisie and Beth. They gasped and put their paws to their mouths. In the excitement of their meeting they had forgotten what had happened a little earlier.

A tap on the microphone made them all turn around. King Bailey stood centre stage, paw in paw with Queen Coffee.

"We haven't found another king somewhere have we?" Lola asked Kiki, who giggled.

"Tzus, friends," King Bailey said, smiling broadly, "thank you all for joining with us to remember Nancy earlier and well, someone told us something that made us think of celebrating our lives together and Queen Coffee and I have to be honest, a few years ago we cheated you all out of a Royal Wedding when we eloped to Paris and well, we think the time has come to put this misdemeanour right".

"It is with a song in my heart that I tell you all that, next Spring, Queen Coffee and I will renew our marriage vows right here in Tzu Kingdom and you are all invited!"

Cheers, whoops and applause broke out from everyone gathered.

Chapter 16

Scout Coffee continued her mission and scoured the forest for the tzu she had seen but it was as if he had vanished in to thin air. He couldn't have done though; he was there somewhere and the only way to find him was to launch a rescue. Quickly.

She needed to get some help and she knew just where to find it. She took her beaker and plate out to the kitchen and washed them up, acting calm so as not to raise the alarm at this stage.

"Otis, Otis," she called to her friend, a small tzu who had spent many years as a scout and was exceptionally gifted as a 'meeter and greeter', always knowing just what gift to take along to welcome a new friend to Tzu Kingdom. He was very professional, and Coffee liked working shifts with him.

"Scout Coffee?"

"Oh Otis, I just have some business to attend to, just some tedious paperwork I need to get signed and sealed by Tanner. Would you mind keeping watch over things, young trainee scout Mac is on the North telescope just making sure the older tzus are well and there's nothing to report. He's so caring, it's like he always has a paw around those who need it..."

"Oh yes, young Mac, yes he is a super tzu. He'll go a long way, mark my words. He's an accomplished swimmer too you know".

Coffee nodded.

"Anyway, could you just keep your peepers trained on the West telescope please, I am sure I saw something there

earlier, not sure what, but maybe just keep looking for him...erm...it. Whatever it is".

"Not a problem Coffee my friend, love to help you, always a pleasure, never a chore!"

"Well, I shall be as quick as I can..." she said as she grabbed the rope ladder to jump on.

"Didn't you need some paperwork signed?" smiled Otis, winking at her and turning back to the telescope, smirking a little.

She blushed crimson through her fur and hurriedly went to her notebook, gathering together a few random pieces of paper that she had tucked inside and popping them in to her uniform pocket, unable to meet his gaze.

Otis laughed to himself as she sung her way down the ladder, clearly up to something.

Coffee jumped off the rope ladder and closed the door quietly behind her, she had to get to the Rescuer Den and she didn't want to raise the alarm. Scouts and Rescuers worked closely together but it was rare for any of the scouts to visit the Den, and vice versa.

She ran quickly to the corridor without alerting any of the Welcomer Tzus and sped to her destination, her ears flying out behind her and her tail swooshing in the breeze.

She rapped on the door of the Rescuer Den. The sign was quite clear:

RESCUERS ONLY

STRICTLY BARK CODE ENTRY

"Hello? Who's there?"

"It's me Zeus, Scout Coffee, wooo hoooo, hello?"

There was some clanking, a kerfuffle and series of muffled woofs.

"How can we help?"

"Well," she huffed, putting her paws on her hips, "I am not having a conversation hollering through a closed door, thank you very much. I have my singing bark to think of".

She tapped her back paw as she waited, impatiently, her front paws crossed in front of her.

The door opened a crack and Lennon's nose poked out through the gap. Coffee stood on her tip paws to try and see in to the mysterious world of Rescuer Tzus. Lennon mirrored her, blocking whatever was behind him but, in doing so, he left a space under his shoulder through which she could see Zeus, in a full suit of medieval armour and Tanner, wearing a welding mask.

"What's going on in there?" Coffee asked, trying every which way to see past her friend Lennon. She knew that the Rescuer Team were always working on new rescue costumes, tools and methodologies and, well, maybe that was all she needed to know, but she was a scout and therefore curious.

"Well, erm, I am afraid that is classified information," Lennon nodded, a little embarrassed as he would have loved to tell his friend what went on in the Rescuer Den. He held a little candle for her after all. He pointed at the sign and shrugged, to let her know that it wasn't his decision and that he had to abide by Rescuer rules.

Coffee rolled her eyes and threw her paws in the air, clearly perturbed.

"Well," she sighed "I had no intention of poking my nose in your important secret affairs, I just need some help. Meet me in the café in two minutes. I need senior rescuer help please, there's a rescue to be undertaken and it's not a mission for the cowardly".

With that, she turned on her paws, flicked her tail and flounced off to the café leaving a shame-faced Lennon behind her. She might be a Canadian tzu, polite and reasonable, but she wasn't going to be pushed around.

Chapter 17

Just a few minutes later, Lennon, Tanner and Zeus joined Coffee in the café with an order of milkshakes. Tanner passed a strawberry shake to Coffee with an embarrassed smile. She stifled a giggle and started to tell them about the tzu she had seen in the forest.

She didn't tell them about the butterflies in her tummy or the Sirius star on his head, just that he urgently needed rescuing and that he was small, matted and in need of medical care.

"The sooner we can get him down to the Comforter Wing the better, I think. Rousey and Brodie are on shift later and I think he needs their care, being a boy dog," she finished.

The rescuers' faces turned serious. They agreed. From what she had told them, he was in danger and they needed to get him safe as soon as possible. They discussed the team for the rescue and decided that they would invite a newly qualified but gifted rescuer, Phoebe, to lead.

"What does Chief Scout Nancy say of this Coffee?" Zeus asked.

"Well, she doesn't know yet because she is in her regular meeting with King Pierre but it won't be a problem. She left me in charge and I will brief her later, before we go".

Coffee and the rescuers agreed that it was only a simple rescue and that she would come with them as the mission scout, sure that it would get approval from Nancy and King Pierre. They needed to leave as soon as possible, as soon as Phoebe came through her fairy door. Lennon looked at her, mesmerised by her pleading eyes and smiled, lovingly.

"OK, we rescue this evening. Let's bring this chap back to safety".

Coffee was satisfied with the outcome of their meeting and they caught the eye of a waiter tzu to order some sandwiches. But, as they chatted and waited, things took a more desperate turn.

* * *

Otis came thundering through the café, shouting for Scout Coffee, his eyes full of fear and upset.

"There you are, thank dog. Scout Coffee, I have seen a tzu in mortal peril. He's an adult and he's been abandoned, he's in grave danger, he's collapsed, and I left young Mac with a telescope trained on him. He needs rescuing, there's not a moment to lose. In fact, I think we might even be too late".

Coffee gasped and looked at Tanner through a shocked and tearful gaze.

He nodded.

"We need to go right now. Otis do you have the fairy door number? Excellent. You and Mac keep watch.

"Lennon, Zeus – uniforms on and Welcome Room in three minutes. Grab mine too and an extra camouflage jacket for Miss Coffee please. I will call for Ms Phoebe.

"Prepare to depart through the fairy door wall in five minutes".

Chapter 18

As they mustered in the Welcome Room and put on their kit, a burp alerted them to the arrival of Phoebe through the New York section of the fairy door wall. Tall. striking and glossy coated, she quickly realised something was a-paw.

"Lennon what's happening? she asked.

He briefed her and introduced Coffee. It was the first time they had met properly, although they had seen each other in the café several times.

"It is a delight to meet you Phoebe. I have been meaning to find you for a chat - I was hoping you would join Nancy and I at one of our Pamper Nights. We have one planned for next Saturday if you are available?"

"Oh, please call me Feebs, every fur does. That's a lovely invite Deputy Chief Scout Coffee but, erm, I am not a very girly girl...but it would be nice to have a chat and maybe a little cake..."

"Oh Phoebe," she whispered in response, "it's more than just pampering, it's where we get to discuss important things, current affairs, with no boys allowed. Fur curlers optional!" she winked.

Phoebe giggled behind her paw and nodded. She knew she was going to get along with Coffee, she always thought she might.

Lennon coughed loudly, and the new friends turned to him, giving their full attention. Phoebe knew there was no time to waste.

"Lennon, it's too late for you to brief me fully so I think it is more sensible if I jump through and wait by the fairy door to see you all back safely. I can keep watch for bad humans and count everyone back".

He nodded.

With that, they were ready, and they jumped through to see if they were in time to save the little black and white tzu with the Sirius star mark.

* * *

Lennon and Tanner landed first and looked around, followed by Zeus. He ran on ahead to look for the tree where the tzu was slumped. Despite having just three legs he was one of the fastest in Tzu Kingdom and, with a skilled nose, he excelled at tracking.

He didn't have to run far; the fairy door was only a dozen trees along from where the tzu was seen and they took comfort knowing that Mac and Otis were in Scout Tower keeping watch.

Looking around and taking account of their surroundings in a dank, gloomy wood full of old twisted trees and thick undergrowth, Tanner and Lennon followed him leaving Coffee and Phoebe on rear guard action, as arranged, with the little scout wringing her paws.

It was quiet, eerily so, the only sounds they heard were the crows up above and their paws breaking twigs as they ran.

Lennon returned, defeated, with a heavy pace and his head bowed. He bit his lip.

"We're too late, he's gone..."

"Noooooooooo".noooooo" screamed Coffee and started to run towards Zeus and Tanner.

Lennon grabbed her around her middle and held her tight in his paws.

"Lennon Lennon," she sobbed as she squirmed and wriggled, "let me go...unpaw me..."

"Coffee my darling friend it's just too upsetting...Zeus and Tanner will make sure he is found, by good humans..."

"Lennon, I think I fell in love with him the minute I saw his kind eyes, even if he's gone I can at least kiss his bonce, smooth his fur and close his eyes for the last time just so he knows he was loved as he looks back from the Rainbow Bridge..." she sobbed.

He put her down and comforted Phoebe as they watched her run to the little tzu. Seeing Coffee hurt and upset like that simply broke their hearts.

She pushed past the boys and threw herself to her knees in a pile of cold, dark, mushy leaves and they stood back to let her say goodbye.

She knelt forward and smoothed his matted fur out of his eyes, so he could see his way. She arranged his white Sirius star marking on the top of his head the best she could, gently combing it with her claws.

"Oh, my Mr Sirius Star...I wonder what we would have been together if we had just got here a little sooner".

Her tears fell on to his face as she leaned in to kiss him.

But those tears, enchanted with fairy magic from jumping through the fairy door in to the human world, stirred him and he opened his eyes and smiled, meeting her gaze once again.

"Hello gorgeous one," he muttered.

She gasped and felt his paw wrist. She watched his tummy rise up and down as his breathing got a little stronger and felt his pulse race as she turned to her team and swished her ears.

"HE'S ALIVE! MR SIRIUS STAR IS ALIVE!"

Chapter 19

Lennon sighed as he sat Paddy and Stanley down in a quiet corner of the Welcome Room. He strummed his acoustic guitar and his long fur flopped down over his face, covering his little sun spectacles.

They had asked him about his time at a rescue centre in Kent, the same one that had housed Elle, Bentz' mother, before she went to her new family. They looked at each other and grimaced, in their excitement they had underestimated the trauma he had experienced as a puppy.

"Sorry Lennon, we did not mean to make you melancholy," Stanley said, reaching his paw out to Lennon.

"You's always so strong pal," Paddy piped up. "We never think of you as getting upset and stuff".

"I just try never to think about it boys. It makes me sad. When I was a puppy, I had a home, but it didn't work out. I was the first to be homed from my litter because, well, I was just about the cutest little tzu you ever did see. I was doted on, for a while, just a while. Then, I suppose the novelty wore off and all of a sudden, I found myself in the shelter reception with all my things − I didn't even get to say goodbye to my children because the woman took them out for the day - and the man telling them how the children were allergic to me. But you know the irony of that don't you fellas?"

Paddy and Stanley shrugged their shoulders and shook their heads.

"You can't be allergic to shih tzus. Technically we have hair not fur".

"So, they made it up?" Stanley gasped. "They told a fib?"

"...and the children must be wondering where you are?"

Lennon sighed. "Yes, and one of them, the little girl, Sabrina, was really lovely. I used to sleep in her room on her panda rug all cosy. I suppose just thinking about Bentz and his mother, it just brought it all back".

He looked up, trying not to cry. He supposed Sabrina must be in her twenties now, she might even have a tzu of her own. He hoped she was happy.

"But it worked out for me, as you know. The Rockstars adopted me the next day and I have never looked back! I get to go on tour and appear on stage – maybe it was just meant to be..."

He looked wistful, he did indeed have a terrific life with his parents whom he referred to, simply, as 'The Rockstars'! They were in a tribute band and he had something of a following himself, with his own twitter account as '@RockStarDogLennon'.

"Anyway boys, how can I help?"

Although still feeling a little uncomfortable, they started to explain that they needed to break in to Battersea Dogs Home in Brands Hatch, from where Elle had been rehomed. They needed to know the layout, so they could plan their mission and find out where she had gone to.

Lennon looked at them earnestly.

"I can't help boys. Since I was there it's had a major refurb. Back in the day it was just wooden pens, but they've spent some money on it and now, well, it's a different place. It's been all poshed up with fantastic halfway homes for dogs and cats. I don't think I would even recognise it".

"But I know two little ladies that were there recently and got up to all sorts of hijinks before they found a home. In fact, I think they even made the papers with their shenanigans!"

The boys stroked their beards and all of a sudden remembered the recently found twins that they had welcomed to Tzu Kingdom on the training day just a few months ago.

"Millie and Bella!"

Chapter 20

The new puppies were trying to remain calm as they ascended the rope ladder to Scout Tower for the first time.

Stanley had come to meet them in the Welcome Room and directed them to climb up. Young and nimble they reached the top in no time at all and he followed on behind, closing the door safely behind him with a bark code and winking at Lennon sat at the desk as he did.

Millie and Bella were star struck. They had met Stanley before when he accompanied Sammy and Percy to their meet and greet when they first found out about Tzu Kingdom. They were also familiar with Winny and Beth, who rushed forward to meet them as they landed on the concourse. They had been in a tidy team with the pair at their first Tzu Kingdom party, parcelling up the leftover food into foil and Tupperware for the next day's lunch and sweeping the stage, much to Queen Coffee's delight.

But today they were to meet Chief Scout Paddy and Maisie, Curator of Tzu Gallery and Chief Librarian. Usually chatty and enthusiastic, right now they could barely muster a woof.

They had made sure they were looking their best. Stanley had popped through their fairy door the previous day and told them he needed their help on a special mission, that they were not to utter a word to anyone - especially in the café - and they were to meet him the next morning. So, they made an early start, brushing each other's fur, cleaning their teeth and shining their collar charms for this big occasion.

However, the warm welcome extended to any tzu or visitor was prevalent in Scout Tower, just as it was everywhere else in the Kingdom. They looked around in awe at the telescopes pointing to all points on the compass, to the ledgers all around that held the names of every known tzu, at the windows to the world outside and pointed up at the photographs of former Chief Scouts, including Queen Coffee and, before her, Nancy.

Winny took their paws and ushered them over to Paddy, sat at his desk with Maisie. Whilst they chatted away, Stanley went to the kitchenette to fetch and carry over a jug of juice and some Tzu Bakery cookies, freshly baked and delivered that morning. He wheeled in an incident board with some coloured pens and joined the meeting.

Millie and Bella held paws. This was a very special day and they were just about to find out why.

Paddy cleared his throat for his formal welcome.

"Well, Bella and Millie, welcome to Scout Tower and a top-secret meeting of the 'Lemonade Mission'. The details are only known to the five of us and we can only tell you ladies what you need to know, on a need to know basis when you need to know it".

"Yes, we have to find Bentz' mother," said Stanley, putting his paw to his mouth as he realised he had said too much.

Everyone laughed, breaking the tension as Maisie raised her eyebrows at her boyfriend and made her sister Beth giggle. He wasn't the subtlest of tzus!

"Oh, I didn't know that was the secret bit..." Stanley confessed, embarrassed.

"Don't worry Stan, the girls won't say a word, will they?" Winny reassured him, looking as stern as a cute, wrinkle nosed tzu could.

The girls shook their heads. Millie raised her paw in the air to ask a question. Bella looked on in admiration.

"Excuse me, erm, Chief Scout Paddy, sir, umm, Lord Paddy, umm, his royal tzuness...Paddy the great...ummmmm".

Paddy smiled a kind smile.

"Paddy, just Paddy".

"Well, umm Paddy-just-Paddy, how is it that my sister and I can help? We don't really know an awful lot...ummm...ummm..."

"Oh, let me explain. You see we need to get our paws on some information, so we can find Bentz' mother and that means we need to pop in to somewhere, somewhere there are no fairy doors, unnoticed, without raising any suspicions and somewhere that you know well. Battersea Brands Hatch, from where you were rehomed".

Wide eyed, the girls gasped excitedly as Maisie gave them two coloured pens each and guided them towards the incident board. It was time to hatch a plan.

Chapter 21

Once they got over their nerves, Millie and Bella were soon in full swing and gave the Lemonade Mission everything they needed to know to get the information.

Although there were no fairy doors in rescue homes, vets or boarding kennels in case a tzu should get stranded in such a place, the Brands Hatch centre was set in twelve acres of fields and there were communal fairy doors, one at the end of the woodland trail. Paddy and Stanley knew them well, they had dropped off a few tzus-less-fortunate there in order to find them a new home. It had always happened very quickly too; the cutest dogs were easy to rehome and there was always a list of people wanting to make them a forever home.

Thursday would be the best day for the visit. The girls had explained that the centre was shut that day, so the only humans around would be the staff and some volunteers. They remembered how this was always a good day to catch up as the computer would be on and the staff would be updating records and adding photos of the new intake.

It was also the day that maintenance and cleaning would occur, so there would be a window cleaner's ladder propped up against the wall, meaning a nimble tzu could easily get to the air vent in the roof and in to the office.

"Well," said Winny, leaning back in his chair happily and taking in the plan that had been drawn on the incident board, "it looks like we have a plan to find my best pal's mother at last!"

They thanked Millie and Bella for their help and, giving them the rest of the cookies to take back home and making them paw promise to keep it a secret. Maisie saw them down the rope ladder and through to their fairy door before returning, with a worried look.

"What on earth is the matter," a concerned Stanley said, running to Maisie, "you look like you have the weight of the Kingdom on your shoulders..."

Maisie sighed and flopped in a chair, draping her paw over her forehead.

"There's a flaw in the plan, I just realised. You see, if the staff are working on the computer then how are we going to find the records on there? They will see us surely? We can't just push them out of the way".

"She's right Paddy, maybe we need a rethink?" Stanley asked, with his paw around Maisie.

Paddy jumped up and went to the Incident Board, with a look of cunning.

"I have it covered, don't panic. You see...Winny will be here, in Scout Tower, masterminding the operation on the Special Ops scope. Maisie and Beth will be here," he put crosses on the board showing their locations, "...and Stanley and I will be here".

The team nodded.

"Well, then temporarily I will be HERE, causing a diversion. We have a young lady in the Comforter Wing, Mitzi, and she is due to be released to a centre in the next few days to find a forever home. Well, if we take her there on Monday, she will be there on Thursday and she can help us create the diversion we need, giving us just enough time to get the records and skedaddle. Plus, I can check the fairy door is working OK when I drop her through".

"Oh Paddy, you are the best!" Beth yelled, running to hug one of her heroes. He blushed and ruffled her fur.

Stanley whistled and applauded. His best friend really was the best Scout, that's why he was in charge.

It was all systems go, a plan was planned and just needed the approval of King Bailey and Queen Coffee and everything would go ahead.

Chapter 22

Coffee pushed open the door to the room where Mr Sirius Star was recovering from his ordeal. She was carrying a tray with a jug of juice, some sliced orchard apple and a slice of toasted, buttered brioche, hoping he would be tempted to eat and drink a little more today.

When she had returned the day after his rescue, things were quite bleak. Brodie took her to one side, explaining that he was an extremely sick dog and they would try their best, but she was to prepare herself for the worst and take comfort in the fact that, if that happened, at the very least he had found love in his final days.

She understood, but she wasn't going to give up without a fight.

Nancy had given her leave and Otis was to step in to her position for as long as he was needed with young Mac, the new scout, taking on some extra responsibilities.

Each day she had come to the Comforter Wing in her most cheerful dresses and brought her patient food and drink.

She plumped his pillows and chatted, making him comfortable and holding his paw whilst she helped him sip, at first, water and then a gentle broth. He had no strength to bark but his kind, wise eyes smiled at her every time she walked in.

Today, she had been told he was a little stronger and had finished off the cream soup she had made yesterday. She was so looking forward to seeing him and felt so relieved. He wasn't out of the woods yet, she knew that, but one paw step at a time...

"Mr Sirius Star, it's me Miss Coffee, I have made you a little toasted snack and some pumpkin juice today...we have to build up your strength handsome!" she giggled.

He was sat up today, looking tiny in the huge four poster bed but smart in a striped nightshirt, and he smelt divine after having another soothing bath earlier with the help of Brodie and Rousey. He hadn't woofed anything yet, but he looked a little stronger, they informed her as they updated her.

She set down the tray and proceeded to straighten up his bed around him, pulling the bedsheet taught underneath him and plumping his duvet. He smiled and sipped the cooling, fruity, flavoursome juice his nurse had prepared him. He looked forward to seeing her, it made him strong, something worth waking up for.

All clean and brushed, he felt so much better and the comforters had brought him some books, magazines and crosswoof puzzles to work through. He had been reading Stella Scholar's inspirational biography of King Leo, the first ruler of Tzu Kingdom, that had appeared at the foot of his bed one morning. Sweet, kind Brodie had brought him through a soft toy to comfort him when he had his bad dreams, a small lion that was amongst his favourite things, not his favourite toy Tigger, but a special one nonetheless, and it sat on the pillow next to the patient as a constant companion and a reminder of how brave he had been.

"Doooo be dooo, tra la la..." Coffee sang as she worked.

"I've been thinking that we should think of a new name for you. I can't go on calling you Mr Sirius Star now! But I just don't know what you like. I mean I suppose we could call you Star or Leo after our first King or there are classic names like Fluffy or Spot or Scooby or Bob or Bernard but, I don't know, none of them seem to suit you.

"It's funny, when I arrived as a puppy with Momma and Dad well, they wanted something unique and Dad had this crazy idea of calling me after their favourite coffee chain and Momma just said "NO NO NO" and stomped her foot down! So, they compromised, Coffee was a lovely name they thought, and I have cappuccino eyes and coffee coloured fur so, that was me...Miss Coffee Shih Tzu...oh you know Bailey is a name that might suit you... it just popped in to my head, Momma and Dad have Coffee with Baileys...or maybe the other way around...on Saturday night after dinner and they call it Bailey's Coffee...I mean not that I am yours or you are mine or anything like that, I mean we are both tzus of the world, independent furs, it's just that well, I feel quite the bond with you, everyone else had almost given up when we found you and well, oh maybe I am just a silly and we should call you Trevor or Kevin or something..."

She turned away embarrassed and faced the nightstand to retrieve his apple.

A fluffy warm paw grabbed hers, tight.

"Bailey," said Mr Sirius Star in a croaky voice, his first woof since his rescue.

"I want to be called Bailey. Coffee's Bailey. Bailey's Coffee. Either is fine by me, just as long as it is for always".

Coffee's eyes twinkled with happy tears as she nuzzled in to Bailey's soft. warm fur.

"Yes, yes, for always," she sniffled.

Chapter 23

The news that the poorly dog had a new name and was starting to recover well spread quickly through the Kingdom and soon, King Pierre arrived at the Comforter Wing with Nancy. Mabel and Myrtle, the comforter sisters, ushered them in to the room where Bailey and Coffee sat chatting and laughing, paw in paw.

Nancy gasped at the sight and nudged Pierre. He walked forward to say hello and Coffee jumped up and curtsied at the tzu ruler.

Bailey made a move to rise from his bed, but Pierre put his paw on his shoulder, motioning for him to stay, and instead they shook paws.

"Such a delight to meet you Bailey, such a delight. Coffee, mon amie, excellent work in persevering and bringing your Monsieur Sirius Star back to health! Look at him, he's going to be just fine".

"And it looks to me like you two are in love?"

There was no denying it.

Bailey felt a little embarrassed, lying tucked up in bed with a fluffy lion whilst he met the King, and Pierre seemed to sense it.

"Bailey, you have been through such an ordeal, we thought we were going to lose you. That hasn't happened in a very long time, the furs we rescue have, mostly, gone on to find happy forever homes and we hope that will happen for you, in time, when you feel well enough. You have taken a big paw step on the road to recovery yet there's still some way to go. So, settle in, make this your home for a while and relax, you are perfectly safe here. Oh, I see you have a lion of bravery too, that will aid recovery for sure. And what smart nightwear".

"Also, Bailey, I can see your eyes are wise, kind and full of knowledge due to your experience before you were found. All the evidence suggests that you were a puppy farm dog, something that is becoming a real issue for the tzus around the world and, before you forget your past experience as I hope you will when good and happy thoughts and experiences fill your head, it would be useful for me to know more about your former life so, I wonder, would you do me the honour of joining me for lunch next week?"

"ME?" Bailey responded, shocked, "I would be honoured".

* * *

A few days later, Bailey walked slowly to the Royal Chamber with Rousey holding him up gently. He was offered a wheelchair but no, he said he wanted to walk and as long as he had some paw support, he would make it.

He was looking dapper. He had borrowed a waistcoat from Lennon and a tie from Zeus. Originally, Tanner offered him a suit, but it was too large so, with a little alteration, they decided on a waistcoat. His ears had more bounce, his fur was softer, and his eyes had more sparkle.

Coffee had tucked a neatly folded handkerchief in his pocket as he left, telling him to have the best time and that she would be changing his bed and bringing in some new books whilst he was at lunch.

"But you must not overdo," she said as she kissed the top of his head, "tell King Pierre when you feel tired, he will understand".

They arrived at the Royal Chamber and Bailey sat in a chair outside to catch his breath. Brodie looked him over, smoothed *his now short fur into a neat centre parting, combed his beard for him and, finally, passed him a flask of water.*

As he watched him sip it, Rousey thought how proud he was of what the Comforter Team had achieved. It was their biggest accomplishment yet and he couldn't believe how well his charge looked, given the terrible state in which he had been found.

"Well, it's 1pm. Are you ready? Shall I knock?"

Nervously, Bailey stood as Rousey knocked and the door was opened - by King Pierre himself.

"Bailey, Monsieur Étoile de Sirius, come on through to the Royal Chamber. The table is all set".

Chapter 24

"....and so that's really how the Kingdom works these days..."
King Pierre concluded, having told Bailey about the promise
made to the fairies many dog years ago.

"It's incredible," said Bailey, looking out of the Royal Chamber
patio doors to the world in front of him. He watched the
waterfall, admired the wildlife and the flowers, the ice rink
and ski slope in the distance all under a stunning blue sky.

He looked up at Scout Tower, wondering if Nancy, Mac or Otis
were on shift today and waved. It was so high he couldn't see
them wave back but he hoped they would see him and laugh.
He thought of Coffee working up there as Deputy and made a
note to tell her not to let him hold her back, she should return
to her post soon, even if just on reduced shifts and now he
was getting better, they could do more fun things.

To his left he could see the path down to the Rescuer Den
and to his right the Party Room, Library and Tzu Gallery.

"Thank you for telling me about your experiences Bailey," said
the King, as he followed his new friend out with a dish of fruit,
jelly and ice cream for him, "it has helped me to understand
so much more about the bad humans".

Bailey sat at the patio table to enjoy his dessert.

"That's ok, but the strange thing is, it wasn't that long ago,
and I seem to have forgotten a lot of it already. It's like it
happened to another tzu, I can speak of it but a lot of the
pain I felt has gone...?"

"Oh Bailey, nothing gets past you! There's an enchantment
over the Comforter Wing, an enchantment that takes away
the pain. The memories are still there, but they are gently
softened whilst you recover. In time, they fade, and you will

only come to think of what happened to you as 'before' and it won't hurt like it once did, being treated badly by those you thought loved you. The fairy spell strengthens the new memories, like the ones you have made with Coffee, and it weakens the bad ones. When my forefur Queen Sally commissioned the Comforter Wing, she asked the fairies to enchant it so and, they did, willingly, knowing this was part of the promise that King Leo had made in the beginning".

The new-to-the-Kingdom tzu listened, entranced, and he needed to know more.

"Who's Queen Sally?"

King Pierre smiled.

"The third ruler of Tzu Kingdom. I don't suppose she ever expected to be Queen, but the situation presented itself when King Wolfgang disappeared, never to be seen again. She took the throne until he returned but he never did. See, she was his friend and his confidante, much like Nancy is to me. She made an amazing contribution, introducing a special place for the rescued to recover".

"So Nancy and you, you're not a couple?"

"Non," he replied, "we are the closest of friends. That's how we like it... come, let me show you something...and there's something I want to ask you too".

They returned to the chamber and King Pierre went to his desk and passed some framed photos to Bailey.

In the first one, was a picture of Nancy and Pierre at a Christmas party with Coffee and a young Soft Coated Wheaten Terrier dog dressed in a red and white coat. Bailey felt a little pang of worry and turned to Pierre with a puzzled face.

"That's Santa Paws Shay Bailey, a good friend to Tzu Kingdom. You know I think he might have had a little soft spot for Miss Coffee but, up until now, she had no truck with suitors, she liked to work hard and play hard but boys? No, it was about fun and dancing, not romance...what have you done to her?" he laughed.

The second held a photo of Pierre with an older female tzu and another of the same age, almost identical to him.

"That's my mother, Queen Mirabelle. Much loved, adored and sorely missed. She ruled before me. The other, that's my brother, Serge. We all lived together in our apartment outside Paris. Then it was just Serge and myself, until a little while ago when he closed his eyes for the last time..."

"Oh, King Pierre, I am sorry...I didn't..."

"Il est tel qu'il est, comme il a été et comme il le sera toujours..." Pierre mused, wistfully, to Bailey's confusion. "Oh, I am sorry, I slip in to French when I am preoccupied...it means 'It is as it is, as it was and as it always will be' mon amie, and that we all have our time on this planet and it teaches us to make the most of it".

Bailey nodded. This made sense. King Pierre was amazingly wise.

The King passed him another frame, this time with a mature Pierre hugging two small tzu puppies.

"That's Franc and Centime, my new brother and sister. They will be joining us here in Tzu Kingdom when they are old enough, quite soon in fact, and they already are destined to carry on our work in the Comforter Wing for, in a few years, Brodie and Rousey will retire".

Bailey stared at all the photos and realised what Pierre was hinting at. Every fur had their time, their purpose and one day *it would come to an end but, still, he didn't understand what this had to do with him. He was just a visitor.*

"I have been on this throne for many years Bailey and, one day, a new tzu will rule us. Today, I have benefitted from your knowledge and experience and I feel richer as a king. You have made me a better tzu you see, I have been lucky. Adopted in to privilege with my brother and cared for by Maman, Papa and Mother Queen Mirabelle. The Kingdom needs a tzu that has known the reverse and I would like to ask you to be my permanent assistant Bailey as we are moving in to worrying times now. Dear Nancy wants to scale back her activities due to her responsibilities at home and, well, you, with Coffee by your side and, soon, as Chief Scout, would be ideal".

Bailey was dumbstruck as Pierre continued.

"You don't have to agree to anything just now Bailey, talk it over with Coffee, get better, have some fun, be a dog! But keep this offer in your thoughts and, once you are settled with a human family, let me know. You will be here a while yet my friend and please, call me Pierre".

"Merci d'avoir confiance et croire dans le royaume - il est plus grand que nous tous".

He didn't translate this time, but changed the subject quickly, wearing a wry smile.

"Well, I think it's back to the Comforter Wing now Bailey, build up your strength a little more and, next weekend, we have a little treat stored up for you! Nancy and I have been planning something - for you to spend some time with Coffee...at her home in Ontario, Canada. She's just moved you see, her second year by the lake and, well, I think a day on the water on Coffee's boat would do you the world of good!"

So much had happened today that Bailey could barely take it all in but, Pierre's last revelation had knocked him for six with excitement and anticipation.

"Coffee has a boat?"

Chapter 25

"No, no, Winny," spluttered Paddy, laughing as he tried to remain standing, holding on to Stanley, who was also laughing with tears running down his face, "'CAMOUFLAGE' not 'CAMEL FLARGE'!"

They both lost it and flopped on to the floor of Scout Tower in a heap, banging their paws, barely able to catch their breath.

Winny looked at them, giggling but still confused.

"So, you're not dressing up in a camel costume to break in to the dogs' home?"

"They're going to Kent Winny, not the Sahara," Mac - now aware of the mission planned - informed him as he also tried not to laugh whilst writing his updates down in the ledger. It was too late, Mac's head went down on the desk, his whole body shaking as he laughed and guffawed in to the book.

Beth and Maisie appeared from the locker room, all ready to go in their disguises and looked at each other, bemused.

"What's happening here boys? Maisie enquired, smiling at the hilarity before her and picking Beth up to see the scene more clearly.

"Well, I didn't quite understand," Winny confessed, "when you were talking about your camouflage gear well, I thought you were going to go in dressed as camels. I was just trying to work out who was going to be front end and who was going to be back end..."

"What did you think 'flarge' meant?" giggled Beth.

"I thought that might be the humps". Winny spluttered, barely able to get the words out before he too slid off his chair!

Every tzu in the room was doubled up in hysteria, it was one of those lovely moments that you can never repeat, a special moment that unites friends.

Chapter 26

Matters had got very serious by the time Paddy and Stanley came out of the locker room, neck to paw in black, finished off with a pair of sturdy boots. Beth and Maisie wore the same but with safety gloves too.

"Wow you look the part you four!" Mac said in admiration. "But pals, are you sure we don't need a rescuer team too? It's quite rare for scouts to head off on a mission without back up".

Paddy huffed, puffed and nodded.

"I hear what you're saying Mac but, this is an information gathering mission, a scout mission, it's not really something that we should bother the rescuer team with. They're planning a big rescue right now, more puppies in peril to save, I mean it just seems like trivia – we just need some information from the computer and Mitzi will cause a diversion when I give the bark and we won't be gone very long".

Mac looked at them all and sighed. It was unusual, and he had been a Scout for a long time. but Paddy was in charge now and he had brought in some great new ideas so, he trusted him. Maybe it wasn't how Coffee or Nancy would have done it in the old days but, well, things move on.

"OK, well I shall be right here doing checks if Winny needs me whilst he's on the Special Ops scope. But King Bailey and Queen Coffee signed this off, yes?"

"Well yes, they know about the Lemonade Mission," Paddy responded. He hadn't said, specifically, that it was a Scout-only mission but he knew that would be fine. Probably.

Stanley smiled, knowing they could rely on Mac to be in charge whilst he and Paddy went on a mission. Winny was a great asset to the scout team and excelled at 'special ops'.

They high pawed each other and climbed down the rope ladder, two at a time. In their camouflage wear with their belts and ropes they really looked the part as they jumped through the fairy door to the field near the rescue centre.

They burped and ran to the back of the tree in the field by the woodland trail. It would be easy to run down. It was quiet, there were volunteers and staff returning from the early morning walks with the dogs looking for homes in their smart 'Adopt Me' coats.

With stealth, they crouched down in the long grass, keeping their plumes low, Paddy at the front, leading the mission, followed by Maisie, then Beth and Stanley at the rear, making sure the girls were safe.

As predicted, a ladder was propped up against the wall and they ran up and gathered at the start of the air conditioning tunnel above the ceiling.

Paddy and Stanley checked their harnesses and climbed up, waiting at the top for Maisie and Beth.

The girls tugged at the wires; Stanley was attached to Maisie and Paddy to Beth.

"You sure you're not going to drop us?" Stanley asked. They raised their eyebrows.

"You are both perfectly safe in our paws. We are strong and focused on the task ahead," Maisie replied, convincingly.

Stanley looked at his friend as they prepared to start their mission and snorted a giggle out as he noticed his bright red accessory.

"Pads, you still have your ear muffs on pal!"

"Can't be too careful," he replied, "I'm a martyr to me ears as you know. It'll be cold in the tunnel and I'm not ending up at the vets for a day having them plucked inside and de-clogged of wax again, thank you very much indeed". He shuddered at painful memories.

Paddy was a character and a great Chief Scout, but he always listened to his Mam on health and safety matters.

Carefully, quietly, they removed a ceiling tile and below they could see a staff member working at the computer. The very place from where they would get the information about Bentz' mother.

There was to be no more talking, whispering and paw signals only.

They were all set.

Chapter 27

As planned, Paddy crawled along the ceiling to alert Mitzi in her kennel. Once again, a ceiling tile was moved, and Paddy tapped it to alert her.

She waved at him and winked. She knew what to do. She had to count to ten and then start to cry, bark and whimper until the member of staff ran out to help. All the other dogs would join in with the barking frenzy until the team were safely away.

Paddy returned and nodded to his friends. As he did, Mitzi started with the noise. It was terrifying. The staff member ran out of the office and as she did, Paddy and Stanley were lowered down to the computer, suspended on a wire with their back paws floating in the air.

They swung down, and Stanley started to search the records. So many times, he had spent his days helping Mama in the office on the big computer and now was his moment to shine. He searched and searched through thousands of records whilst Paddy kept watch through the office door.

The dogs waiting for their forever homes were going bonkers! As soon as one stopped woofing another barked relentlessly until it got some attention.

Stanley worked away on the computer, pressing keys and clicking the mouse whilst the staff member went from kennel to kennel, observed by Paddy through the glass panel in the door.

"Got it! I just need to print this off," he whispered, "it's an email from the magazine people and it tells us exactly where Elle went to live!"

Paddy smiled and gave him a paw-thumb up from the door but then did a double take...Stanley wasn't at the computer any more...he was spread-eagled just centimetres from the office floor.

* * *

"EEEEK" Maisie cried.

Beth swivelled round as her sister let go of her wire, with Stanley attached. She grabbed it with her back paws before Stanley plummeted all the way to the ground.

"What? What?" Beth said to a trembling Maisie.

"SPIDER!"

"Maisie, you're not scared of **spiders,** are you?" she exclaimed, shocked that her brave-as-a-lion big sister who rescued her from a puppy farm on a dark and cold night was scared of anything at all.

She nodded and whimpered. Beth wasn't afraid though; she had spent her first few weeks of life in a nasty shed with her mother and their friends and it was full of spiders.

"Squish it squish it!" screamed Maisie.

Beth shook her head.

"No, no one gets squished on my watch. 'If you wish to run and thrive, let a spider run alive'," she said, repeating words she had heard their Mummy Megan say as she had explained that everything had a right to live, even if they weren't your cup of tea. Clearly, this lesson had escaped Maisie and she felt ever so grown up, helping her big sister.

Despite having Stanley hanging from her back paws and Paddy from her front paws and in danger of all three of them landing on the floor in a heap, Beth summoned all her strength and turned to the spider happily trundling towards them.

"Mr Spider, Mr Spider," she called, "hello, Beth the Tzu here, is there any chance at all that you could return home as we are terribly busy now and in a precarious predicament and my sister appears to not be a fan of your kind, but we wish you no harm. We shan't be much longer..."

The spider stopped suddenly, looked at Beth before turning on his eight little hairy legs and returning to whence he came.

Maisie breathed a sigh of relief and grabbed the wire from Beth, hauling a rather shocked Stanley back up to desk level, recovering her composure, if a little shaken up.

* * *

"What on earth is going on up there?" whispered Paddy, as Stanley moved back up and grabbed the printed email from the printer.

"I think it's best not to ask," he whispered back.

Stanley was worried now, he wondered if he was a little too heavy and decided that he needed to get fit when he got back. It was time he put his new FitBark to good use and start to get in shape. He might not be a rescuer, but scouts needed to keep fit too. A gentle jog each morning would do it. He would post a note on the noticeboard in the Scout Tower kitchenette to see if others wanted to join him.

They turned their noses up to the ceiling and gave the signal. They had what they came for.

"UP UP UP!" said the boys.

Maisie and Beth winched Paddy and Stanley back up in to the ceiling with Stanley clutching a piece of paper in his paw.

"Well?" Beth said, hopefully.

He held the email out for them all to read. The plan had worked a treat and they gasped as they realised where Elle, Bentz' mother, was. From reading the email exchange, they deduced that she was clearly having a great life on a beautiful island with a family that loved her to the moon.

"We'd better tell Mitzi to stand down," Paddy laughed. They had not needed to be quiet as the dogs in the kennels had all been taking it in turns to bark, keeping the member of staff very busy and right out of the office.

"I'll tell her," Beth shouted as she scuttled across the roof to shout down to Mitzi Tzu. But, in her excitement, she miscalculated and her sister and friends could only watch in horror as she fell through the ceiling tile and into a pile of freshly laundered bedding below.

"Well, hello, little tzu, you must be Mitzi," the kind kennel lady said to Beth. "I don't know how you got out, but let's get you back in your kennel quickly".

Chapter 28

Maisie gasped. This unfortunate mishap and resulting case of mistaken identity was not in the plan, it had all gone horribly wrong. She looked from Stanley to Paddy, and from Paddy to Stanley.

They looked at each other, and then back at Maisie.

Paddy strained his neck to see what was going on. Beth was sat still in the middle of the kennels and all the dogs had gone quiet as events unfolded. It seemed that the kennel lady was looking for the right key. Beth couldn't bark in case the lady was enchanted and she would hear her speak and the entire cover for Tzu Kingdom would be blown.

It was a pickle for sure.

"Ok," he said, trying to hide the fact that he was panicking like he'd never panicked before, "let's not panic at this stage and look at the facts".

"There will be confusion soon when the door gets opened and she sees that Mitzi is inside ok so, they will probably run a chip scanner over both shih tzus to see who is who, right?"

Stanley looked relieved. "Oh, the wonder of the microchip, reuniting lost dogs with their loving families...of course...it gonna be ok Maisie...Maisie..."

She shook her head. She felt sick to her stomach.

"She's not chipped yet. She's booked in for her big girl operation next week and the vet lady is going to do it then and..."

Her eyes filled up with tears again. This was scarier than the spider.

Stanley gripped her paw; he had no idea what to do now. It had turned from an information gathering exercise in to a rescue mission. He felt out of sorts and terrified that Beth would never get home.

Paddy felt equally frightened, he wished that he could turn back the clock and ask Phoebe what to do, he should have sought her knowledge and advice.

He chewed his lip. He had to step up now and rescue Beth but he was a Scout, with no rescuer training and he was scared out of his fur. His experienced colleague, Mac was right, they should have involved the rescuers, even just for back up. The only other option was to leave her behind and hope that Mummy Meghan would find her here but, in seven days, she could be rehomed somewhere else and never get back to her real home.

And it was all his fault.

They sat silently for a moment when a crash sound from behind made them all jump.

"Move over scouts, this is a rescuer job!" Alice shouted as she ran down the tunnel, in full rescuer gear, swooshed past them and over to the ceiling above Mitzi's kennel.

She threw a rope around a pipe and abseiled down the kennel wall, scooping Beth up in her paws and snapping the rope back to her hip.

"Hold on tight kiddo!" the brave rescuer shouted as she ran to the office, swung the door open, jumped up on the chair and sprung on to the desk.

"ROPE!" She yelled, making Maisie throw the wire down. She grabbed it and whistled so the boys hoisted the pair of them up.

"SCRAM!" Alice squealed, running past them super-fast. They ran after her, back through the tunnel, down the ladder, across the field, along the woodland path and straight to the fairy door. The girls jumped through but Paddy stopped sharp.

"My muffs! My muffs!" He shouted as he and Stanley went to jump through. They had fallen off and were laying half way down the path.

"I'll get them..." Stanley cried heroically as he ran back to retrieve his pal's attire but as he got nearer, he could see humans coming towards him, after what they thought were escaped dogs. They were good humans but he didn't want to explain to Mama, Dad and Granny how he ended up in Kent after just popping out the garden for a sniff. But he had to get Paddy's ear muffs. He just had to.

"Leave 'em Stan, Mam can buy more..."

But Stanley wasn't listening, he could do this. He could save the day. He was as brave as a lion.

The humans were just metres away from the muffs and, with all his courage, he ran towards them, grabbed them in his teeth and sped away from the path in to the long grass, slowing down the people chasing him. He ran further, towards the fairy door, re-joined the path and threw his paws around his friend.

Paddy barked for the fairies to open the door again and they were safe, all five of them in the safety of the Welcome Room of Tzu Kingdom. The boys were laughing but then they looked up and the girls most certainly weren't. Beth was crying and Maisie was comforting her. Alice had a face of fury.

It had always perplexed them before but now they knew why she had the nickname of 'Fierce Alice'.

Alice turned to Chief Scout Paddy, with her paws on her hips. She looked furious.

"We need to talk mister".

Chapter 29

Mac was also pulling a stern face when the team arrived back in Scout Tower, his paws crossed across his chest.

"Thank dog Winny is on the ball with his Special Ops duties Paddy. He knew you were in trouble with all the time it was taking and alerted me, so I ran and found Alice and sent her through to rescue you".

Winny smiled, he knew he had done the right thing, but he didn't mean to get Paddy in to trouble.

"Thank you, Alice. You saved the day and no mistake!" he said, trying unsuccessfully to start a round of applause.

Maisie settled in the Scout Tower sofa with Beth now in her paws, cuddling her as she sobbed uncontrollably, her fur soaked through.

Stanley had never run so fast in his life and he was just coming to terms with what had happened, but he didn't like an atmosphere, so he tried to get things back on track.

"Well, we are all back safe and we have what we need so, shall we have a debrief?" he grinned, heading towards the incident board to write up some notes.

"Debrief? DEBRIEF?" Alice screeched. "DEEEEEE. BRIEEEEEF?"

She raised her eyebrows and threw her paws skywards.

"Paddy, Stan, you should know better than this. Especially you Paddy...YOU ARE SUPPOSED TO BE **CHIEF** SCOUT!"

They shuffled their paws and looked down at the floor, red-faced.

"What if Bentz found out one day that one of his friends got lost trying to find his mother? He would never get over it".

Silence.

"AND what, just, WHAT was the delay? You were right behind us and then you were gone?"

"Erm, Paddy's ear muffs fell off so I went back for them," Stanley smiled, thinking he might get a commendation for this incredible act of bravery.

"Muffs? You put yourself in danger again over some EAR MUFFS???!!" Alice screeched as Stanley wondered whether he should put them on himself to save his hearing.

She continued, never looking away from them once.

"We are a TEAM here in Tzu Kingdom are we not? Rescuers and scouts, welcomers and comforters, café staff and bakers. Is this not the key message that King Bailey and Queen Coffee try to get across to every single tzu that jumps through the fairy doors? The most important message that King Wolfgang took back to olden times? Well?"

Stanley gulped, red-faced and upset.

Paddy stepped forward; his head hung low.

"You are right Alice. I should never have tried to carry this out without working with the rescuer team. I guess I just felt I wanted to show off a bit. I thought I could handle this without a full team, without rescuer input. I forgot we were all spokes in the same wheel".

"I have made a terrible mistake. Queen Coffee would never have done this, or Nancy before her. I put my best friends in danger and an unchipped tzu in mortal peril. It doesn't get worse than that".

"All I can do now is tender my resignation as Chief Scout".

Chapter 30

Rousey jumped through the fairy door followed by Bailey and then Brodie. They all breathed in the fresh lake air and admired the lush trees all around that fanned a gentle breeze around them and made their fur flow and their toes tingle.

"Mmmmm Canada". Rousey exclaimed as he breathed deeply and then burped, taking the air right down in to his lungs as he restored to full size, "you just can't beat the Lake Ontario air..."

"Is this why Coffee is so beautiful?" Bailey asked, his eyes sparkling as he looked around, a large burp taking him by surprise.

"I think it's certainly part of the reason," Brodie burped in agreement as they all grew back to normal size after shrinking down to jump through from Tzu Kingdom.

Bailey looked at a sign in the distance next to a row of pretty boats. 'Rice Lake', he read as he admired the gleaming vessels and the cool, shimmery blue water on which they sat. The white boat at nearest to him caught his eye and on its side it read 'Lady Latte of the Lake'. He knew just who this belonged to and smiled.

"OK, Bailey, Rousey and I are going to leave you now. Coffee and her Momma and Dad are heading down, they will be here any minute so just watch and once they are parked safely, let her know you are here and there should be a good day of sailing ahead for you two love tzus!"

"I will be more than fine Brodie, thank you. Oh, and it was very kind of the two of you to leave those boating books for me on my bed, I have read all three of them from cover to cover".

They looked at each other, they hadn't left any books on Bailey's bed.

"OK, so you are clear which tree has this fairy door yes? You know how to get the fairies to open it?"

It was Bailey's first time jumping through the fairy doors on his own. He had had a couple of practices this morning.

"Bark loud and firm," he answered, sagely, "and the kind fairies will let you through...if you're tzu!"

"Thank you, I shall return to my bed chamber in the Comforter Wing as soon as we dock this evening".

Rousey and Brodie barked, waved and jumped back through.

For the first time since he had been found all those weeks ago, Bailey stood alone. He thought about his new friends and his beautiful room in Tzu Kingdom with his lion stuffie, books and outfits and realised that, just as King Pierre had assured him, he could barely remember any details about what had happened to him before. A little hurt and upset stirred in his tummy but he wasn't going to focus on it, he was happy to forget, even though the memories were there somewhere.

He was glad because he knew that a new adventure was just beginning and that Miss Coffee Shih Tzu, Deputy Chief Scout, was at the heart of it.

Chapter 31

For a few minutes, Bailey sat on a fallen log and admired the view across Rice Lake and beyond to Lake Ontario. It twinkled at him, as if it was giggling and inviting him to splash and play and he smiled back. As he began to laugh, he heard others join in and then he saw a white car heading down the hill to the harbour. He heard Coffee and her Dad singing as they got closer to him.

He stood and watched as they parked up and disembarked. They continued to sing as they unpacked a bag of food and their sailing essentials.

Coffee shimmied with her human dad, her ears swinging in the breeze, and then she ran to Momma and held her hand with her paw as they kissed and waltzed around the dock. Momma and Dad were both tall and they picked her up to dance for a while, eye to eye and smile to smile. It was the first time he had seen a real family doing family things.

Bailey was mesmerised but it was time to make his presence known. He tip-pawed down to the boat dock and stood on the landing next to it and looked on as Coffee skipped along, regularly looking back to check that her family were near her still.

He hoped he had dressed appropriately in his shorts and Hawaiian shirt, borrowed from the irrepressibly cool Lennon. He wondered if he should wear formal attire for a first proper date but no, Nancy had assured him, dress for the occasion and you can't go wrong.

Otis had visited to give him a fur cut and had fashioned his thickening coat in to a short style, with a plume of glory, a smart beard and his ears now hung in the fashionable

"BoyBob" - the current craze amongst many of the male tzus, especially the ones called Bob.

He straightened his shirt and brushed the creases out of his shorts with his paws. It was time to surprise Coffee with a greeting.

"Hello Pawjuss!"

Coffee stopped singing and dancing as she jumped in to the air.

"BAILEY! MY BAILEY!"

Chapter 32

Coffee could hardly believe who was stood in front of her. She grabbed his paws and they danced in circles, laughing as they twirled. They stomped their paws with happiness and hugged each other tight.

"Bailey, my love, what a lovely surprise. I mentioned to Nancy how I would like to take you sailing...will you join us today? We have a picnic packed and lots of treats that I would be delighted to share. Momma always packs far too much!"

"Oh my darling I would be honoured, it is everything I have dreamed of! A date with you on the water, sailing and singing!"

"Well, let's get you kitted out and I will introduce you to my family".

Momma appeared behind Coffee; her face full of curiosity.

"Coffee do I hear a voice?" she looked around but shook her head, 'it must be the sun making me hear things' she thought and put her bag by her feet, pulling a stylish sunhat out and placing it on her head.

Her tzu daughter giggled and whispered to Bailey, "don't bark anything more than a whisper for half an hour, you're enchanted from jumping through the fairy door and Momma's enchanted too and can hear you because she's all relaxed!"

Bailey made a lock and key sign across his mouth and winked.

"Oh, Coffee dear, you seem to have found a little friend...hello young man where are you from and where is your family?"

She leaned down as Bailey stood, bowed and then offered his paw to his new human friend.

"Delighted to meet you..." Bailey said, forgetting he was supposed to be quiet. Momma shook her head again and reached for her water bottle, supposing the heat must really be getting to her today.

Coffee laughed and turned away. Bailey made her quite the mischievous little fur at times with his funny ways.

"Jeff," called Momma, "Coffee has a little shih tzu friend here, come and meet him...he's adorable".

"Who's Jeff?" Bailey mouthed.

"That's my dad," Coffee replied, "those are their names in the human world and, well, you will need to call them Ms Barb and Mr Jeff because, of course, only I am allowed to call them Momma and Dad," she responded, looking a little upset.

"Of course darling," he whispered, "I shall address them appropriately," he smiled as the happy look returned to his love.

He turned to Coffee's dad and held his paw out to greet him.

"Well, who do we have here? We haven't seen you before little man. Welcome to our dock and to Rice Lake," he said in the friendliest of fashions as he shook Bailey's paw.

"He seems to be all alone here and I don't recognise him," said Momma, looking around, "do you think he's lost?"

"He doesn't look lost Barb and I think we would have known if there was a missing shih tzu anywhere in Roseneath ...someone would have rung us, maybe even thinking it was our Coffee or that we knew him, being Tzu Parents".

"Well, what should we do, I don't want to leave him here alone whilst we are on the boat because I'll worry and look at Coffee, they seem inseparable...almost as if she knows him. I think she might have a crush".

"Could he come with us do you think?"

"What if someone is out looking for him?"

They hummed and sighed, looking around. Finally, Coffee raised her eyebrows and shook her head.

"I honestly don't know how they would cope without me..." she said as she went to Momma's bag and leafed through it with her paws, tossing out tissues, snacks, phone, dog treats, a money purse, card case, hand gel, mints, jelly tots and mini fan until, eventually, she surfaced with a notepad and pencil in her mouth, dropping them, assertively, on Momma's feet.

Bailey mused how she was very much the same dog as she was in Tzu Kingdom here in the human world.

Coffee tapped her paw until Momma looked down.

"Oh Jeff, I have an idea," she hollered at her husband as he wandered about looking for any people who might know the mystery tzu, winking at Coffee, "we could leave a note at the entrance saying that if someone is looking for a handsome black and white shih tzu with a star marking on his head that they are not to worry, we have taken him out on 'Lady Latte of the Lake' and will be back early evening".

"Well done Momma, excellent idea 'of yours'," Coffee said as she rolled her eyes, making Bailey snigger.

"Barb," said Dad, "what are we to call this little fella for today?"

She thought for a minute. A lovely name had popped in to her head the previous week when she was gardening with Coffee, tending to the tulips.

"Let's call him Bailey for today, it suits him".

"I told you Momma was enchanted," Coffee remarked, proudly, to a shocked Bailey as she swished her tail and strutted off to her boat.

Chapter 33

Aboard the boat Bailey was fitted out with a smart lifejacket - Coffee's spare. He was safe and happy with an inflatable bowl of fresh bottled water to share with his sweetheart.

They stood at the front of the boat as they prepared for departure, paw in paw, enjoying the cool breeze.

Momma spread a towel out for them both to lay on in the sun and another in the shade. They were set to sail.

As the boat sped up their ears and plumes fluttered in the breeze and Coffee went over the safety rules.

"Now, Dad is Captain Jeff, and the rule is you do whatever he says. Boating is fun, but there are dangers so you must obey. Also, if Dad – Captain Jeff – delegates to his First Mate then you do what she says, OK?"

"Oh, is that First Mate Ms Barb?" he asked, nodding.

"Nope," Coffee replied as she adorned her head with a white and navy cap, 'First Mate Miss Coffee Shih Tzu of the Rice Lake Canadian Navy SEALS...at your service!"

She snapped her heels together, stood tall and saluted.

'Hubba Hubba', thought Bailey, completely awestruck, his knees as weak as the first time he got out of bed in the Comforter Wing.

* * *

"Is my little darling girl coming for a dip?"

Coffee jumped up and leaned over the side to where Dad was swimming whilst the boat was anchored.

"Back in five minutes," she shouted and, without further warning, she dived off the boat with an almighty splash.

Bailey gasped and ran to the side where Momma caught him by the lifejacket.

"Hey hey little man, I don't even know if you can swim," she laughed, stroking him as he wriggled in her arms, "look Coffee is just there, swimming with her dad, having fun!"

He looked down and to his relief, there she was waving at him as she swam with Captain Jeff holding her gently with her ears floating, fanned out on the surface of the lake as she bobbed up and down.

"Phew," he said.

"I'll take him for a quick swim," said Dad, - Barb, please can you cast off 'Coffee Island'".

Momma went to the back of the boat and Bailey followed. She unleashed an inflatable circle that she pushed towards the swimmers.

Bailey wasn't sure about this swimming idea but, before he knew it, there he was, floating on the lake with Coffee and Captain Jeff swimming beside him. She climbed on to the island and shook herself dry as he was lifted down in to the water, safe in kind human arms.

He flapped his front paws and kicked his back legs and, supported around his middle by Captain Jeff, he was swimming.

"Woooo hoooo Bailey look at you!" Coffee shouted from her island.

He felt so proud of himself and so happy. Here he was, a dog from a sad and lonely before, swimming in the sunshine in a stunning Canadian lake with his love and her family!

"Feel the fear and do it anyhow!" Momma shouted from the boat.

"I'm on top of the world!" Bailey bellowed, powering through the cool blue water.

Chapter 34

Lunch was delicious. They had eaten together on the deck on the back of the boat, drying on a towel. Momma had brushed them both through after their swim, dousing them with fresh bottled water so they were squeaky clean of lake water.

They had stood and looked out to Sugar Island, a real island on the lake, holding paws but now they were nearly dry and enjoying an ice cream as their ears dried in the sun. Tzu ears always took ages to dry and Coffee showed Bailey how to shake them properly.

As he finished his ice cream, Bailey decided it was time to talk about the future.

"I'm starting a little job next week darling," Bailey informed Coffee.

"What? You're not going to overdo and make yourself ill, are you?" she said, full of concern and worry.

"No, no. I'm going to do three shifts a week at Tzu Bakery. You see, I am nearly always up early and I take a stroll and well, I had to find out where the amazing smell was coming through so, I followed it and it led me to the bakery where they were baking bread for Tzu Kingdom and other dog worlds. Well, I was invited in to join them for the morning and I thoroughly enjoyed it so they asked if I wanted to be a baker and I thought well, yes, it's time to repay the kindness of Tzu Kingdom with a little paw work. So, I have signed up to do two mornings a week on doughnuts and an afternoon shift on cupcakes. I shall be taught to ice them as well as bake. You can never have too many skills," he said as he touched his paw to his nose.

Coffee nodded. She would worry about him but he was getting better and he needed to do something to make his way in Tzu Kingdom. Three shifts a week was about right and Cherie, chief baker, she would keep an eye on him, especially if she had a little word with her over a milkshake.

"And there's something else darling...you see King Pierre has asked me to help him, to be his key advisor and assistant. Pierre believes in succession planning and he knows he is in the autumn of his life. What's more, as you know, Nancy is going to have to be at home more with her human father and he feels I can offer him insight in to the terrible ways that some dogs are treated. Most of all, however, he wants to ensure that someone can pass on his ruler skills to the next King or Queen of Tzu Kingdom and, I don't know why he would choose me but, well, he said to believe in the Kingdom and I trust him. Coffee darling...do you think I should do it?"

Coffee considered this for a moment, but she had something to get off her chest too.

"Bailey, I think changes are a-paw. Pierre has asked me to take over as Chief Scout as Nancy has decided to retire. I really want to do it; I am so honoured to be asked. What do you think?"

He smiled.

"I think we both know the answers in our hearts, don't we?"

She nodded back.

"I wonder who I will be tutoring to be the next ruler of Tzu Kingdom," Bailey reflected as he thought about his role more deeply. He sat up, startled.

"Coffee, as Chief Scout, it could be you!"

"Me? No, no, not me, a little fur like me? Queen? Perish the thought, the Kingdom would be in bits!" she giggled.

"Well, I'd vote for you," Bailey said, bowing low to her.

"Silly Bailey," she said, kissing his bonce.

They finished their ice creams and laid back on the fluffy towel, kicking their back paws in the air.

"Bailey, there is talk of a home for you in the next few weeks, has anyone spoken to you about it?"

"Yes, Pierre himself mentioned it. A lady called Karen, in a faraway, sunny land called Essex, in the countryside where zebra shoes are worn".

"That's her, we are just working out how to get you there you see, she isn't in the best of health and doesn't think she is up to having a dog but, well, that's just nonsense! So, we will find a way. You will need to look after her as well as she looks after you but I think it will be wonderful, you will bring out the best in each other. She has a big black and white cat called Dillon; he will protect you both".

Bailey was sure this was the family for him, but he didn't want to think about it too much, in case it didn't happen.

"Coffee, how did you find your Momma and Dad?"

"Oh well that's easy. I came to live with them as a puppy. They had been together, and married, for some years since Dad turned up at Momma's office one day on his way to a party, dressed as a clown. They went out to dinner, then they were wed, then they bought furniture, Momma bought hundreds of pairs of shoes, went out for more meals, went on holidays and took pictures, then they decided to get me. Well, that is when their lives really started and we moved from our apartment in Toronto to the big house here in Roseneath so I could have a garden to play in rather than the big park. I got a new fairy door installed in my cedar tree and then boom boom rah rah here we are on our boat!"

"Why was Captain Jeff dressed as a clown?" Bailey puzzled.

"Erm, to impress pretty young Momma I would imagine," she replied. She had never really thought about it before, that was just their story.

Bailey reached for Coffee's paw.

"Will you marry me?" he asked.

She gasped and her paw flew to her mouth.

"Oh Bailey, what a wonderful thing to ask me, wonderful, but we don't need to be married. We love each other and will be together for always, getting married is a human thing with documents and things, I'm not leaving you ever! Hardly any furs get married, we just don't need to, our bark is our bond".

Bailey had a tear in his eye. "Are you sure that's enough?" he asked her.

"Oh, it's more than enough and more than I ever dreamed off".

"Well, OK, if you paw promise to never leave me".

"Paw promise," she promised.

Paw in paw they sat, happier than either of them ever thought possible.

Chapter 35

Alice sighed at Paddy's offer to resign.

"Oh Paddy, don't be a nincompoop! No one wants that! Sure, you made a mistake, but we have to learn from that, OK? Now, Stan is quite correct, we need a debrief".

"We don't need to tell Coffee and Bailey either, they must have assumed you had involved the rescuers so, we just see this as a lesson learned right? I got there, it's all going to be just fine".

She hugged him tight, he loved being Chief Scout and he thought about the Tower and his role all the time. This was just a hiccup. If you never made mistakes, how would you ever learn?' she thought. She had scolded enough and the boys had listened to the voice of experience.

"Stan, you have to learn too. Ear muffs, well they might seem important but they are just 'stuff'. They can be replaced, you and Paddy can't. I mean, I know you rescued Millicent the teddy bear when we rescued Maisie but that was a little different, Maisie wouldn't leave without her".

Stanley sniffed. He just wanted to be a hero in Paddy's eyes. "I'm sorry Alice, I know, Pads said to leave them and that his mam would get him another pair but I saw them lying there and...well..."

Paddy put his paw out to his friend, he already thought of him as his hero, he didn't need to retrieve his ear muffs to be his most special friend in all the world.

"It's ok pal, but family and friends are more important than stuff. Anyway, I am on me third pair as it is, me Mam got them in the pound store...I think there's more in me and Mitch's things cupboard anyway. You're much more important

100

than stuff. Never risk yourself like that again. I am so sorry I put you all in danger. I love you Stanley me BFF!"

They hugged tight and everyone smiled, breaking the tension at last. Beth giggled and blew her nose on a tissue from Maisie's pocket, wiped her eyes with her paw and was all smiles again.

It was going to be alright.

Winny coughed to attract attention.

"Would you like me to make some sandwiches in the kitchenette? We can't work on empty stomachs after all," said the sweet, small shih tzu with big loving eyes, covering the special ops telescope over for now, mission complete.

Everyone nodded, he was spot on!

"Alice, as our guest up here in Scout Tower, would you like cheese & ham or ham & cheese?"

"Oh, ham & cheese for me please Winny," she replied.

Winny skipped off to the fridge. He wasn't surprised, he had a feeling she would be a ham and cheese tzu because Bentz and he also took their sandwiches that way and he was pleased, because she had just started paw-stepping out with his best friend.

He could never understand why anyone would have cheese & ham, but he guessed it was just the way you were brought up. But it just seemed wrong to him.

He listened to them chatting whilst he buttered the bread, happy that it was all calm again and eager to hear about what they had discovered.

Chapter 36

The sandwiches were delicious. Alice cleared the table of knick-knacks, cups and plates, giving a sideways glance at Paddy as she went to get a damp cloth to wipe up some spillages from today and, clearly, some time before. Winny brought a dry cloth through too and dried the table off whilst Mac quietly and diligently continued his shift and Maisie snuggled Beth on a beanbag, snoring gently in unison.

Paddy looked at Stanley, embarrassed. They really had to start keeping Scout Tower tidier. Stanley remembered when he first met Phoebe after his first night in Tzu Kingdom and had been in her 'tidy team'. He decided, there and then, that he would put a checklist out for each shift, making sure everything was tidy for the start of the new one and everyone taking responsibility.

She spread out the email, arranging the pages in to a neat order and scouring the text for an address.

"Scouts," she quizzed, "I don't quite understand. They say Elle is going to live on an island, but it seems that they will still be living in the Great Britain, but then they talk about the weather in France and getting a ferry?"

The boys climbed up to the table and studied the email.

"Well, there are a few little islands dotted around the UK Alice, but they're talking about the weather and how close it is to France, you're right..." Paddy was confused.

Something popped in to Stanley's head. He knew where they were, and it made him glad that he listened to Mama when he was at his work station.

"The Channel Islands!" he said.

Chapter 37

Stanley unfurled the map and weighted it down with a mug in each corner, much to Alice's amusement. She would source them some paperweights from her catalogue, as a little treat.

With his paw he pointed to a scattering of tiny islands. Mama had a client who had become a friend and she lived on Guernsey, one of the big islands. Word was that, one day, he would fly there with her and enjoy a break by the pool with Hamish, the dog of the house.

Stanley showed them how close they were to France and that they enjoyed the warmer weather from mainland Europe. There were two big islands – Guernsey and Jersey – and then the smaller islands Alderney, Herm, Sark, Jethou and Brecqhou. There were others too but they had no people on them.

Alice nodded. "I think we are beginning to narrow it down and we have to look for clues in this email".

Paddy jumped up, mug in paw. "Let's look for things that might help in this conversation. Stan? Could you wheel the Incident Board in please?"

They went through each page of the email strand diligently, Alice neatly circling anything that might help whilst Stanley wrote it up on the board and then stood back.

"So," said Alice, stroking her silky beard, "we are looking for an island that has two halves, linked by a bridge, no cars, a windmill, millions of beautiful butterflies and a dark sky".

"Well, that rules out the big islands, they both have airports," mused Paddy.

Stanley thought long and hard. This was starting to sound familiar. Mama had talked about a day trip to a little island on her most recent visit and that she had stroked a horse's nose. 'Which one? Which one?' he thought, feeling the island's name swirling somewhere in his brain. He closed his eyes to make himself think harder, he knew he knew.

"Stan...you OK?" Paddy asked, prodding him.

"I think he's in a trance...what's he singing?" Alice asked, concerned.

"GOT IT!" he yelled, punching the air with his paw!

"I made up a little song when Mama told me about her visit! It's the dark sky...my song goes....la la la...'Sark is dark, but a butterfly's light...Sark is dark, but a butterfly's light...' and I sang it out in the garden when I saw a cabbage white!"

"SARK! Elle lives in Sark!"

Chapter 38

Within a minute, Mac had the telescope trained on the one fairy door in Sark. Butterflies danced in front of the view of the waves crashing on to the shore.

There was only one fairy door on Sark now, the population of the island being so small. Others had been sealed up until a time when they were needed.

Paddy looked through the scope, mesmerised, as Mac explained.

"It looks like Elle and her family live on the other side of the island so, we will have to send a small mission – maybe just a scout and a rescuer – to find her. As it happens, there is a record of an ancient fairy door where she lives now so we would have to make a request to the fairies to re-commission it if Elle wants to visit her children, and vice versa".

"It's just gorgeous," Paddy sighed, "it looks proper romantical..."

"Hey, I have a neat idea!" Alice ventured, putting her paw on Paddy's shoulder. "Why don't you and Phoebe go, make a day of it. It would be wonderful if you do something together and Stanley will hold the fort with Mac, won't you boys?"

Paddy needed a break; he had been working so hard since he took over. Some fresh ocean air and a chillax amongst the cheerful flowers would do him good, as would spending some time with his girlfriend Phoebe.

The boys nodded. Of course, they would do anything for Paddy. He had got upset earlier and needed to recharge his mojo.

The Chief Scout blushed, muttered his acceptance and cleared his throat. He looked at Winny, Maisie and Beth fast asleep on a beanbag.

"Well, we had better get these sleeping beauties home hadn't we Stan? Alice, thank you for all your help today. We wouldn't have got through without you my lovely friend".

Now it was Alice's turn to blush, although that was a completely correct statement.

"So, allow us to see you home too please, paw in paw".

"I would like you to feel welcome at Scout Tower in future and, I suppose, that you would like to return the favour and invite us for a visit to the Rescuer Den sometime soon?"

Alice burst out laughing.

"Nice try Paddy Chief Scout, but that not gonna happen!"

Paddy shrugged at Stanley as Alice climbed down the rope ladder, still laughing.

Chapter 39

Bailey looked in the ornate French mirror in the Royal Quarters, hardly able to believe it himself.

"Hello, King Bailey!" he said.

He turned and looked around at his office. Overnight, comforters Mabel and Myrtle had cleaned it beautifully and it smelt like a summer meadow.

If a little bare.

It was almost a month since King Pierre had closed his eyes for the last time at home, with his family all around. Since then, Bailey had kept everything running well in the way he had since becoming his assistant and, as Pierre's health had deteriorated, he had taken on more and more of his duties.

When it came to electing a new ruler, no other tzu threw their names in the hat and, when nominations closed the previous evening, there was just one name put forward with endorsements from every senior Tzu.

His.

He looked around the office stood atop a stool. He was smaller than King Pierre and he had to climb up just to see himself in the mirror. He didn't look or feel any different in fact, he felt just about as little as he ever had, and a little frightened. He moved a little step stool to the mirror.

The Royal Chamber had an oak desk with a swivel chair for its occupier and, on the other side to the mirror a stunning throne, engraved with the names of every King and Queen since Leo. Tomorrow, his name would be added.

At the back, a corridor led to a bed chamber, rarely used but available to a visiting dignitary. The corridor continued along to Tzu Gallery and Tzu Library.

Behind the large desk were a set of patio doors that led to a private garden surrounded by a low stone wall where, some years ago, he had enjoyed a lunch with Pierre when he first arrived. From here you could see all of Tzu Kingdom, a telescope bringing the furthest reaching elements in to view.

He looked at the crown case in the corner, the Tzu King's Crown under lock and key. He knew it would be a little big for him so it was to be enchanted by the fairies overnight and, by tomorrow, when the past King's nearest and dearest – Franc and Centime – placed it upon his head it would be a perfect fit.

Could he really be King? Could he pull it off? One thing was for sure, he didn't want to do it alone.

Chapter 40

A knock at the door shook King Bailey out of his daydreams.

"Come on in, it's open," he hollered.

"Your Majesty," Zeus said as he bowed.

"Zeus! What's all this??!!" laughed the new King, "stand up stop being a silly fur...I am still Bailey, your pal!"

Zeus shook his head. "No, King Bailey, you are more than that now. You are part of history, the ruler of our world".

"Well, maybe just call me KB then, that's a little friendlier. In fact, it's a name I wish all my close friends to address me as...erm, is that something I can decree...?"

"It sure is KB, you're in charge!" laughed Zeus, bringing through a bag of costumes. "We rescuers gathered together the wigs, noses and shoes you asked for this morning...are you sure about this?"

King Bailey nodded. "Yes, the formalities start tomorrow yet, there is one thing I must do before I am crowned".

*** *

"Knockity knock...Oh Majesty King Bailey...may I come in...?"

"Sweetpea! Darling!" Bailey exclaimed as Coffee poked her nose around the door of the Royal Quarters.

She curtsied, beautifully, but he took her paws and helped her back up.

"No, no, none of that, I just don't want to be THAT sort of a King...Pierre never was and I never shall be. I am still just one

109

of the tzus of Tzu Kingdom...I just somehow ended up with the big job!" he laughed, with a twinkle in his eye.

"I agree, you must rule in your style...the furs elected Bailey and well, that's clearly who they want. Oh Bailey Bailey Boo, this is so exciting! Just to think I am the girlfriend of the King". Little Miss Me! I promise to remain faithfully by your side and I am always here to bark with and relax with, K?"

He knew. It was forever and always. He held her tight and she giggled before looking around them.

"Well, I think It's time to Bailey-ize these rooms, don't you? Pierre always said to make it personal to the ruler so I have a few things in my office in Scout Tower, I'll just run up and get them. Be right back," she called over her shoulder as she ran off down the corridor.

Bailey had a little surprise of his own and he headed off to the bed chamber where he had stashed Zeus' bag of tricks under the bed. As he pulled them out, a floorboard squeaked and when he looked, it was a different colour to the others. He would investigate that when had had time, but not now, he only had a few minutes.

As he stood up, he noticed the window was open and as he closed it he admired the view of the gardens and looked up to Scout Tower, one of his favourite places. He saw two small girl tzus running towards the waterfall, holding paws, one girl smaller than the other. 'I shall look after every one of you he thought,' smiling at the girls' unusual attire and thinking they must be sisters.

He opened the bag and pulled out its contents, pulling them on over his own clothes. Stripy trousers, polka dot shirt, spinning bow tie, braces, over large shoes, a rainbow wig and finally, the pièce de résistance, a shiny red nose. He had no idea why the rescuer team had all these costumes but he trusted them as Pierre had and he was content to let them continue. Perhaps it was better sometimes to trust rather than over-manage. Same with the Scout team, he would no more tell Coffee what to do than fly! She had it all under control, just like Tanner did, although he wondered whether she would say yes now and become his Queen.

As he finished dressing, he picked up a book from the bedside table - 'The Quiet Hero: King Muffin's Tale' and flicked through the pages. He would read this later he thought and set it aside, to do just that.

He pinged his shiny red nose on and waited for Coffee to return. If dressing as a clown had wooed her Momma then maybe, just maybe, it would work on her fur daughter.

Chapter 41

The King hid behind the door with a bouquet of flowers as Coffee pushed it open by wiggling her back against it, carrying a box.

As the door closed, Bailey jumped in front of her.

"Coffee will you marry me and become Queen of Tzus?"

"WAAAAAAAAAAAAAAAAAAAAAAAAAAAAAAA" she screamed as the box flew through the air. Bailey dropped the flowers and caught the box, stumbling back and landing on the floor.

"Who are you Mr Clown, where's my Bailey?" she cried as she pinned him to the floor with her knee.

"Darling, it's me," he said, "pulling his red nose and rainbow wig off, "your Bailey!"

"Bailey what are you doing, you scared me almost out of my fur," said Coffee, laughing hysterically and rolling on to her back, clutching her sides.

"Well, it worked for Captain Jeff - the clown outfit - so I thought you might say yes to my proposal if I did the same".

She looked at him. The same cheeky, silly Bailey that she fell in love with all those years ago was King now, but he hadn't changed a bit. She loved him even more, but she wasn't ready to be Queen.

They sat up and she looked him in the eyes with a serious look. He smiled hopefully. She took his paws in hers.

"Darling Bailey Boo, I love you to the moon but the time to get married just isn't now. Maybe one day the time will be

right but not today. I will never leave you, paw promise, and my bark is still my bond".

"Scout Tower is so busy, Otis is just about to retire, Mac and Bonz are both taking on new strategic roles and need to start the fast-track programme for new scouts. Things are a-changing and I need to concentrate on that – on my team, for the sake of the Kingdom".

King Bailey looked crestfallen. Coffee had to make this right; she didn't want the first few days of his reign to be marred with sadness.

"But, my love, I have an idea. What if I take over your Assistant Desk and then I have a place of my own in here to assist you and also to have a place to think about Scout Tower without interruption. Oh, and let's move them round so we can both look out to the patio and I will plant up some tubs outside too...see...that's a lovely view to work to, yes?"

He had to admit, as he watched her put the flowers in vases and on their desks, she was right, that was better and, if she was going to work alongside him well, that was nearly as good. Plus, he had something to hold on to. She said 'one day'. He hoped one day soon.

***

Bailey changed out of his clown outfit and returned in a casual suit to find that Coffee had made some significant improvements.

His desk was now full of photo frames; one of him with Coffee at a dance, one of them both with Santa Paws Shay, one of him with King Pierre, one of him with his Mum and their cat Dillon, one of the senior tzus taken at a Christmas party and another of him with Brodie and Rousey on his last day living in the Comforter Wing.

Gracing the tables throughout were scented candles, sparkling ornaments, glittering trinket boxes and plaques with motivational words. The fireplace was decorated with indoor plants and brass statues. On every chair and sofa was an arrangement of cushions and throws and a casual pile of luxury beanbags were placed around a low coffee table, in conversation style, amongst an assortment of furry rugs.

"I'm just finishing the curtains darling, almost done ...there... Thoughts?"

It was incredible, everything was just stunning and looked amazing.

"If you don't mind me saying my little Coffee Cup, it very much feels like home...our home...our happy place. Thank you, I love it".

Paw in Paw they smiled. Content in their Happy Place.

Chapter 42

"The eyyyyyyyyyye of the lion..." sang Paddy and Stanley as they reached the top of 'Montagne Pierre', the large hill at the outskirts of Tzu Kingdom.

The boys danced, whooped and cheered. Finally, they had done it! They had got all the way to the summit without stopping.

Several weeks ago - when they first started their 'Beanbag to Mountain' fitness programme - they could barely make it around the orchard without puffing and wheezing, often stopping to hold on to a tree or sit on a bench. Truth was, they were so embarrassed at their lack of fitness after seeing Alice in action they had to do something. They were Chief Scout and Deputy so setting an example as leaders was important to ensure the scouts remained at the hub of the kingdom, working with the rescuer team to bring tzus-less-fortunate to safety. Plus, they still wanted to eat plenty of doughnuts. Stanley's Mama had been on a similar human running programme and was racing up mountains now so, once he got his 'FitBark' from Granny he thought, maybe, some subtle messages were being wafted his way.

"We are as fit as puppies again Paddy," Stanley declared, performing jumping jacks whilst clapping his paws above his head.

"Yip, up n down the old rope ladder like ninjas...!" laughed Paddy, performing some press ups with one, then the other, paw behind his back.

They both flopped down on the grassy hilltop and breathed in the sweet morning air. Suddenly, Paddy saw something out of the corner of his eye. He sat up and stretched his neck out. At the other side of the slope was something he hadn't seen from Scout Tower – a marquee.

Stanley noticed him look and jumped up, peering over.

"Shhh...listen...I hear banging 'n' clanging...also, can you smell warm honey?"

"Look! It lit up, the tent, there's sparks too...let's go see..."

Stanley hesitated; he wasn't happy about going on a scary mission alone after the ear muffs episode. Paddy sensed his reticence and hesitated too. He heard a whistle and it made him swing round. Approaching the tent from the side of the hill was a familiar face from Paddy's past.

"It's Otis, retired scout...OTIS OTIS!!!" he hollered, running down the mountain, gathering speed at an alarming rate. Stanley followed him, enjoying the breeze in his fur. Paddy and Coffee often mentioned Otis, he was a fur of experience and had the respect of everyone.

Otis jumped when he saw the boys running towards him and swiftly hid something behind him.

"Are you going to that big tent? Is it a secret?" Stanley questioned him, with a grin from ear to ear. They were on to something here.

"Stanley, Paddy, just taking a stroll, enjoying the mountain breeze..."

"With a pot of paint?" Paddy smirked. He winked at Stanley; they had caught him red-pawed.

Embarrassed, Otis knew he had been rumbled. They were wily these two and no mistake, they would go far.

"OK, boys, I am working on something in the tent, that's the truth but, I just can't tell you, it would ruin the surprise for Queen…well, it's a secret".

"Secrets amongst scouts Otis?" Paddy clutched his paw to his throat and gasped. Looking shocked he staggered backwards.

"But what about the 'Scout Code'?"

The older tzu sighed, defeated. "OK, follow me, but I have to clear it with the others first…" and he scurried ahead to the tent.

"Well remembered Pads, I didn't even know there was a 'Scout Code'," Stanley remarked in a whisper, impressed.

"Neither did I pal…" Paddy sniggered, impressing himself with his quick thinking.

Chapter 43

Paddy and Stanley stood outside the tent, listening to the muffled voices inside.

"Can you hear that Zeus with his secrets Stan? I don't know! Once a rescuer, always a rescuer," sighed Paddy, "remember when we went down to the Rescuer Den in our lunch break once to see if Feebs wanted to go for a quick milkshake and we had to wait outside like we were waiting for detention?" he rolled his eyes, making Stanley laugh. He did remember, they finally reached the café to find Maisie there waiting to order, tapping her paw.

A floating tzu head appeared before them. Zeus looked their way, holding the tent doors tight around him with his one front paw, and that wasn't easy.

"Can you boys keep a secret?" he said, sternly.

They nodded and muttered, "...scout code, trusted tzus...scout code...Otis knows..."

Zeus let the curtain door drop, raising an eyebrow and looking from Paddy to Stanley, and from Stanley to Paddy.

"Look, this is a surprise for Queen Coffee and King Bailey for when they renew their marriage vows. It's something that has been missing and in a state of disrepair, rotting away for decades".

"We silver furs, well, we found it in the forest when we were on a nature ramble, it had been hidden there since the days of crazy King Bolan. It is believed that he might have crashed it there and, embarrassed, told his kingdom that it had been lost. Well, we found it...we know Bailey had heard about it from Pierre and, well, it's going to be part of the 'Tzus Renew' celebrations".

The excitement was growing.

"We promise to keep it a secret, we love QC and KB and we wouldn't spoil a surprise for them. Paw promise," Paddy said, saluting Zeus, Stanley quickly following suit.

"OK, well, I guess it would be nice if some furs saw it and we need a test drive so...do the honours Brodie and Rousey..."

The retired comforters swept the curtains back to reveal one of the lost legends of Tzu Kingdom. Stanley couldn't believe his eyes; he and Maisie had read about it in the library just a few weeks ago but, even if you didn't know its history, it was still amazing to behold.

"I can't quite take it in. Is it really the original? Not a copy?"

The silver furs nodded.

"It's not, it can't be..." Paddy exclaimed.

Before them, sparkling with fresh glitter paint, sparkle curtains and liveried just like in the history books with today's rulers painted on the side was an iconic vehicle that had once ferried tzus around the land and, it was rumoured, to other dog worlds too.

The Tzu Kingdom Bus.

Chapter 44

"Watch!" Otis said as he barked and started the engine, "we've bark coded it so it runs on woof commands which means that almost any tzu can be driver. We had this in mind because of Zeus with his missing leg and, well even those who can't see can drive with a pal. You just bark the commands and...hey presto...off and running! Plus, it runs on honey and, take a look at the exhaust. Rainbow emissions!"

They loved it.

Every seat's upholstery had been beautifully recovered and stitched back to its former glory by Rousey and Brodie with 'KB&QC' embroidered on the head rest in silken thread. Within each head and paw rest were lights that changed colour when the engine was running and the seat belts were furry, like a warm hug.

An enchanted drinks dispenser capable of serving any drink requested was nestled on the table between each set of four seats and, in turn, the seats were angled perfectly for shih tzu comfort and conversation.

At the back was a velvet-curtain-enclosed circular Royal area that would allow Coffee and Bailey to work, entertain and relax. They would be travelling in style when they went to other dog worlds on royal visits.

Looking up at the glass roof the boys imagined how beautiful it would be at night when you could see the stars but even in the day it would sparkle gloriously when the glitter ball was twirling.

Outside, the wheels shone with silver sparkly bolts glimmering against the jet-black rubber and the paint work twinkled under the morning sun. The exit had been custom-made too with steps or the opportunity to leave the bus on an inflatable slide.

"You sure have worked hard on this," said Stanley, in awe of what they had done.

"Anything for Queen Coffee and King Bailey," Brodie said, "they deserve it," he mused as he thought back to the time when they first met Bailey.

"We've been hiding it under here and on the side of the mountain so you couldn't see it from Scout Tower," giggled Otis to startled looks from the Chief and Deputy Scout, "oh yes, I didn't spend all those years working with Coffee in Scout Tower without learning a thing or two about where you can hide things in plain sight!"

"We didn't expect you boys to run out this far, to be honest, but I think we are all pleased you did now," laughed Rousey, "but we trust you, keep it under your hats until the big day okay?"

Paddy looked at Stanley and smiled. They both had a lot to learn from their elders, despite their positions of authority and, maybe, it would be a lovely thing if they spent some time with the silver tzus. Stanley had spoken to Paddy about all he had learned from his friend Peter, the elderly gentleman he shared biscuits with when he went on his Therapet visit to the seniors' home and they had thought a lot about elders recently.

"Can we come rambling with you one day maybe?" he asked, to nods from the older tzus, once so crucial in the day to day running of Tzu Kingdom but retired but now, older, wiser and full of knowledge that should be passed on to the younger generations. It was up to them to learn and pass the knowledge on because, one day, they would be the silver furs.

Stanley put his paws in his shorts pocket and gasped.

"Oh no, Paddy look! My FitBark! I meant to leave it in my locker! What is Mama going to think when she downloads my stats for the day! I have only been down to the garden and up to the shops as far as she knows!"

Paddy laughed. "She'll probably be off for a replacement from the shops Stan!"

"Well, you had better not put any more steps or runs on it Stanley," Zeus said, concerned, "so what if we quickly drop you back to the orchard on the bus and you can just run back to Scout Tower from there?"

Never had Paddy and Stan moved so fast - they jumped in to a booth and buckled up for the ride, pressing the candy dispenser for sweets as they went. After all, they had earned them after their run!

Chapter 45

"Colin's going to be OK Bailey, I have just come down from Scout Tower. Bonnie watched as his dads took him straight to the vet. Lola and Kiki jumped through a fairy door near there and they listened outside when one of them called both sets of their parents with an update. He took a nasty kick from the bad human and, well, yes, his leg is broken, but it's a clean break so just a simple operation then it will be rest until it heals. Also, I checked on the way and Paddy has settled in lovely in the Comforter Wing. He will be ready for a new home in days and we have the most wonderful lady in Liverpool in need of a fur, she seems perfect – he's a strong and feisty one, he's had the comforters in fits of laughter! I have promised him he can go up and see what happens in Scout Tower tomorrow, I think he could be on the fast track training programme you know. Oh, and darling I found the Tzu Gallery key on the floor of the Welcome Room so I picked it up and..."

Then she saw him, huddled on the sofa by the window, hugging his knees with his chin rested on them, his ears listless and his face tear-stained. He had been as brave as a lion when Colin had returned injured but now, in the safety of the Royal Quarters, his sadness he could hide no more. She laid the key on her desk and went over to him.

"Tzu Gallery is locked until further notice," he told her, "until Tzu Kingdom can find a ruler worthy of having their portrait hung in there".

***

Today had been the unveiling of King Bailey's portrait and she had been so proud standing next to him as Franc and Centime pulled a little curtain rope and unveiled it to the gathered tzus. It depicted Bailey in his full regalia and crown with a plate of doughnuts on the table next to him, to represent his time as a Tzu Baker, and a cafetière of coffee, for his beloved. He stood under a moonlit sky, with stars twinkling above him as a nod to his Sirius Star marking.

The unveiling had been magical, and a marvellous feast followed, at which the senior team presented him with a state-of-the-art gravy fountain for everyone to dip their sausages in at parties.

Everyone loved their king and everything had gone swimmingly well since he had been elected and crowned. There were lots of celebrations to celebrate a good deal of hard work. The Kingdom band, 'Tzu Aroo', had a new spring in its step and their tunes were sung every day.

The rescuer and scout teams were working together superbly and they had united in their mission to save dogs and puppies from puppy farms, just like Bailey himself was saved.

Coffee was an amazing Chief Scout and she had trained Mac and Bonnie in strategic roles, taking care of equipment innovations and records, respectively.

With Brodie and Rousey retired, Mabel and Myrtle now headed up the Comforter Wing with assistance from Franc and Centime. New baths had been installed to help the rescued dogs recover as they often had terrible skin.

The rescuers were still a slight mystery to every tzu but the rescuers themselves, but Tanner and Lennon had taken charge now.

The welcomers were happy in their roles and Coffee had helped them introduce new furnishings all around with soft cushions bursting with colour and sparkling with glitter.

The refurbished café was working with Tzu Bakery to supply every popular pie, pasty, bread and cake tzus could think of as well as introducing milk shakes and smoothies.

Tzu Library was brisk with book borrowers and Tzu Gallery had visitors seeking knowledge every day.

Tzu Kingdom was happy and successful under King Bailey's rule and he had pleasantly surprised himself too.

But something was about to change.

Chapter 46

The party was in full swing with King Bailey and Coffee leading the dancing with a lively Shih Tzu Shuffle as Mac ran in to Tzu Gallery with news.

There was need for an urgent rescue of a small tzu called Paddy, trapped in a garage by an uncaring owner. The senior scout didn't want to interrupt the fun but the situation had been under surveillance for a few days now and there was about to be a window of rescue opportunity. A lock on the door to his horrid home was broken and they could sweep in and rescue him. It was a tricky one and needed a team of five.

Bailey swung Coffee into Otis' paws so she could continue dancing.

He listened to the story Mac told him and agreed, the rescue should happen now. He beckoned Tanner and Lennon over and they quickly organised a team, calling in Kiki and Lola. They needed one more for and they looked down to see Colin, newly qualified rescuer, grinning up at them with his paw in the air, desperate to be chosen.

A smiling Bailey looked to Tanner.

"What do you think of taking Colin?" the King asked him.

"He's newly qualified KB, I'm not sure, these humans are unkind and..."

Bailey laughed and responded with a glint in his eye.

"Nothing will go wrong Tanner, everything is good! Take the young fellow, he won't let us down. Colin?" he said, turning to the youngster, "Obey Senior Rescuers at all times OK?"

He danced off, catching Coffee mid-twirl and stealing her back from their good friend Otis. Tanner was reticent, but he trusted King Bailey and, after all, nothing had gone wrong since he came to the throne. It would be fine.

But it was just an hour later that Tanner returned with a crying Colin over his shoulder.

Kiki and Lola ran a dazed and confused Paddy down to the Comforter Wing as Lennon explained how the little one had turned back at the last minute and given Paddy's captors a piece of his mind, against rescuer rules. He had been kicked, hard, and something had snapped in his leg.

The dancing and music had stopped and the crowd gathered around as Bailey knelt down to look at Colin's injuries, holding his trembling paw in his own.

"There, there, brave as a lion," he comforted him.

"Let me through, let me through," shouted Coffee as she joined Bailey beside the injured tzu. She wrapped a blanket around him that she had grabbed on the way to try and stop him shivering.

"Sweetpea, I think this is beyond comforter care..." he said, choking back tears. She nodded and held on to the patient as Bailey took control.

He stood, cleared his throat and recovered his kingly composure.

"Tzus, please be brave. Colin is injured and we must get him to where he can be fixed and that lies with his humans. As you know, Colin has two wonderful fathers, Dads and Popsy, and they adore him. Colin needs V. E. T. treatment; his injuries are beyond the enchantment of Tzu Kingdom. It's urgent and we must take him to the safety of his home".

"Otis, Tanner, Mac, Lennon, please carry him through his fairy door and ensure he is found swiftly. Thank you".

They rushed forward, slid him on to the blanket as a stretcher and burped for access to Colin's Notting Hill garden where his showbiz parents would find him.

"Friends, I think our party is at an end today and it is time for home but, one thing I ask of you all," they listened as Bailey looked thoughtful, "young Paddy, the tzu we just rescued, is never to hear of this, it would upset him and he could blame himself when, clearly, this is down to me and me alone".

"It's not your fault King Bailey," shouted a fur from the audience, to a chorus of agreement. He smiled.

"Let's tidy up Tzu Gallery quickly please and then lock it up. This day will not be spoken of again, thank you my friends, my flock, my wonderful tzus".

Chapter 47

"Bailey, what do you mean?" Coffee said as she took his paw in hers, perching on the edge of the sofa.

The sad King looked out of the window and sighed.

"I knew I wasn't up to this, I am no Pierre, no Leo, no Muffin...it's best that I step aside before something even worse happens. It's entirely my fault that Colin has been hurt, no one else is to blame".

Coffee had to be truthful, but she chose her woofs carefully.

"Bailey my sweet, yes, if we are honest maybe you are a little to blame, but not entirely. Colin knew that he was to do as he was told and he decided to turn and bark at the bad man. He did not obey senior tzus. We all have to take responsibility for our own actions, OK?"

"Coffee, Sweetpea, the buck stops here. With me, the King...but I am not worthy of being so..."

She stood and put her paws on her hips.

"Mr King Bailey, I do not imagine for one moment that you are the first ruler of Tzu Kingdom to make a mistake. How do you think King Wolfgang disappeared? Why do you think it took King Muffin so many years to sort things out after the crazy kings? Why do you think Pierre needed an assistant?"

"And Colin will be fine. Maybe he will have to rethink his rescuer career or maybe not – having a leg missing never stopped Zeus and, as Pierre told us both - 'confiance et croire dans le royaume - il est plus grand que nous tous'".

Bailey smiled at Coffee's French barks; she was fluent thanks to her Dad. 'Barksperanto' was the official language of Tzu

Kingdom and every other dog world, but she was educated, and often slipped in to French Canadian language, one of the few that could speak French with Pierre back in the day and, now, Franc and Centime. But he knew this phrase well, Pierre had indeed introduced it to him and he trusted his words.

"Trust in the Kingdom, it's bigger than all of us," he translated, sighing once again.

"You would be a much better ruler than me, you are cleverer, smarter, prettier, with proper papers too, and every fur adores you. Coffee, you must be Queen of Tzu Kingdom, I am going to abdicate in your favour and, maybe, I can return to my assistant role and everything will be well. I just know it is the right thing for the kingdom".

From where she would never know, but a vision of their future appeared in her head and she knew it was time to trust her instincts and trust in the kingdom she so adored.

"You are right Bailey". He looked relieved at her words. "I will be Queen on one condition".

Bailey smiled; he knew this was the right thing. Coffee and him working together, but with the burden of responsibility lifted from his small shoulders.

Yet, to his surprise, Coffee then sank on to one knee and looked up in to his eyes.

"Bailey, King of Tzus, I don't want you to carry all the responsibility of the Kingdom because I love you to the moon, so...please, will you marry me and rule the Kingdom of Tzus with me, paw in paw?"

Bailey could not believe what was happening and he slid off the sofa and joined his beloved on the floor, throwing his paws around her.

"Yes, my darling, yes!"

They laughed together and held each other tight.

"We will rule together, you as King and me as Queen, stronger together...yes?"

"Oh yes my darling, that seems the right thing to do. We will ensure we look after each other and look out for each other, making our decisions together, weighing up all the facts, yes?"

"I have to continue as Chief Scout, at least until there's a tzu ready to take over Scout Tower...OK?"

"Yes, whatever you want my love. When should we marry?"

"How about tonight, Bailey, in the shadow of the Eiffel Tower, in Paris?"

Chapter 48

Nancy was quite out of breath when she reached the royal chamber and she flopped in to an armchair.

"OK," she gasped, "it's all sorted!"

"Franc and Centime will meet us at their fairy door and accompany us to the Eiffel Tower. Louis Battenberg will conduct the ceremony and then it's back to Hotel Battenberg for the wedding breakfast!"

"Centime is organising flowers and Louis will lay on a delicious spread for us all, it won't be much given the short notice, but it will be first class of course, as you would expect from the world's top dog hotel and its world class Canine Concierge!"

"Oh Nancy, I am not worried, I just want to be married, a milkshake would suffice!"

"Oh my little Coffee Cup, you think I, your bridesmaid, will let you get away with anything less? And are you sure you wouldn't prefer a big state wedding here in Tzu Kingdom? I can pull that together in a week with a little help..."

Bailey looked at Coffee with pleading eyes, he just wasn't up to that right now and a week seemed like a lifetime away.

Coffee understood his eyes instinctively and so responded, with empathy for her dear fiancé.

"Thank you, my dear Nancy, but, no, this is what we desire. A simple ceremony - it's more about being husband and wife than having a party. Maybe we will celebrate one day when the time is right".

"King Bailey and Queen Coffee," Bailey twinkled, excited at the thought.

"Gosh, my little protégé is to be Queen Coffee of Tzu Kingdom," Nancy realised, looking at her with pride, "I always knew you were destined for great things".

The grandtzu clock ticked in a quiet moment.

"It's time to go lovebirds!" Nancy declared as she jumped out of her seat.

Bailey and Coffee stood too and made their way towards the door, along the corridor and to the fairy door wall in the Welcome Room where Carmen slept at the desk.

"Sssshhhh," don't wake her, Nancy said as they giggled at her loud snore, "I asked the fairies to do a little enchantment, just so we could slip through unnoticed! She will awaken in a few minutes, bless her little fluffy toes!"

She jumped through the fairy door, leaving them alone for a moment. They looked at each other, they needed no words, this was how it was meant to be.

Holding paws, they jumped through the fairy door to Paris.

* * *

Meanwhile, back in the Royal Chamber, two young tzus code barked their way in via the patio doors.

They had to be careful to leave everything just as they found it, no tzu could know that they had even been here in case that resulted in the bark code changing. This was a tricky mission, the most difficult so far.

"Oww!" said the smaller of the two, stubbing a toe, "who put that desk there?"

"Here, let me rub it better my little smartie and WHISPER! We have to be quiet and quick!"

"I understand Professor, sorry. So, do we change now, in to our smart outfits?"

"Yes, in the back-bed chamber, as soon as I have the...aha...key! Got it! OK, quick like a bunny, in here, change outfits, put the Tzu Gallery key back in the Welcome Room desk drawer and straight through the fairy doors. One more stop before we're done and I drop you off with...well, I shall tell you soon enough!"

Within minutes, the two of them were in their finest clothes and they left the Royal Chamber through the front door, tip-pawed along the corridor and to the Welcome Room, past the sleeping Carmen to the fairy door wall and jumped through to continue their adventure.

Chapter 49

Paddy and Phoebe were both city tzus and used to noise. The first thing that struck them was the quiet.

In a strange way it was deafening; no cars, no sirens, no shouting.

"Can you hear that Feebs?" he asked, "nothing but the sea and the breeze..." Paddy breathed in deeply, enjoying the car and airport free air. It was like stepping back in time.

"I can, that and the clip clop clip clops...look..." she smiled as a horse trotted past them, bidding them good day. "We have horses with carriages in Central Park but they aren't happy, they never say hello, they have to work with traffic and they don't like it. Here on Sark, well, it's a different world for them".

"Oh my! Look a pair of Lappet Moths," Phoebe whispered in an excited voice. She had read all about them in 'Insects of Sark' by WA Luff and was ecstatic, knowing she was unlikely to see one on the streets of New York.

The two senior tzus had done their research and now, it was time to rescue Bentz's mother Elle. They had arrived on Little Sark and needed to make their way across La Coupée to La Seigneurie Gardens where she lived nearby with her family. In addition to telling Elle that her five puppies were alive and well, they were to bring an ancient fairy door back in to use so that she could regularly visit Tzu Kingdom too. They were so looking forward to telling Bentz and his sisters, as well as getting to know her. As they walked along the bridge that linked the two little islands, they smiled at each other and drank in the flora and fauna. They were happy and relaxed walking the two miles in to the larger island, knowing that something wonderful was going to happen as a result of their hard work. Plus, it was the first time they had been together on a date, outside of Tzu Kingdom.

At the end of the bridge they paused together and gazed out to sea.

"Paddy?" a concerned Phoebe ventured, "do you think we are doing the right thing here? I mean, this little island, it's about as close to a human Tzu Kingdom as you could possibly get and Elle must be so relaxed and happy. What's worrying me is that if she's left all the bad stuff behind her, well, what if we just stir it all up again and make her sad. I mean, Bentz and his sisters had such a terrible time and, well, I guess Elle did too. You remember it took ages to coax Bentz out from his hiding place after he arrived and well, what if it's the same for his mother? What if she wants to forget?"

Paddy sat down and pondered. This really was a worry and he didn't know what to say in response. They had come this far, but maybe they needed to turn back and leave Elle to heal, never revealing what they knew.

Paddy had made a few mistakes, he didn't mind admitting, and had certainly learnt about impetuousness and now, a more considered and mature tzu paced and pondered the pros and cons. There was no incident board out here on which to write his thoughts and no sandwiches and cakes to help the thought process. Phoebe and him, alone, had to make an extremely important decision and it weighed heavy on their shoulders.

"Well, I know from what Winny tells me on his shifts in Scout Tower that Bentz prays to the Sirius Star every night that one day he will be reunited with his mother. She's never far from his thoughts. They had a special bond see and I think we can only assume that she feels the same".

"You speak the truth Paddy; Beth has told me the whole story of how they got separated straight from Bentz' own woofs. All

137

I can say, having been Beth's foster mother for a while when we rescued her, is that no matter how it hurt me I would definitely want to know what happened to her if we had been separated, even if it was bad news. I would want to know..."

Paddy smiled and squeezed Phoebe's paw.

"I think we have our answer my lovely lady, it's good news and we have nothing to fear. Even if it brings back the bad memories, they will soon be eclipsed by the news that her five little puppies are well and making lives for themselves. As a bonus, we will be opening the world of Tzu Kingdom for her and, even if we just see her for milkshakes in the café, it's going to add nothing but happy to her life".

Together, paw in paw, they continued their journey to meet Elle.

Chapter 50

They arrived at the gardens and hid behind a large oak tree where Paddy had arranged to meet a charm of fairies to re-enchant the fairy door for Elle. They heard giggling and, after a few seconds a fluttering around their ears and noses.

Phoebe giggled. "Stop it," sniggered Paddy, "we can't be seen!"

Two fairies stopped in front of their faces, smiling at their friends and pointing over to a pond where humans were enjoying music and eating burgers and salad from a barbeque.

"Is it her Chief Scout? Are we to re-enchant?" asked Hector the male fairy, with Abigail, his wife, by his side.

"We need to be sure, haven't seen her yet but I shall give bark as soon as we are sure".

Peeking out from either side of the tree they knew what they were looking for, but nothing looked as they had imagined. They waited, looking slightly forlorn and wondering if they had got it right after all.

"Charlie Charlie!" shouted one of the humans, making their ears prick up. They stood on their tip paws and, to their relief, a motorised wheelchair appeared from the side of the house, expertly driven by a teenage boy accompanied by a shih tzu, the image of Bentz with flowing looks and beautiful eyes.

They had found Bentz' mother.

They watched for a few minutes in awe as she looked around to check her charge was safe, she walked calmly around his wheelchair to make sure there were no hazards and then, on request, removed his hoodie for him as he was a little hot.

Paddy turned to the fairies and nodded; it was time to open a fairy door. He and Phoebe stood back and watched as their wings flapped faster and faster, they twirled around the tree making sparks and zings until a faint smell of burning wood emerged from a blur of fairy activity.

As the smoke cleared, a fairy door shape glowed and within seconds, an ancient entrance to Tzu Kingdom was returned to full glory.

Abigail the fairy touched the bark and the door opened. She returned just seconds later brandishing a small ball of wool.

"It works, Carmen will want this back though!" she laughed.

"We're all done here, all down to you now Paddy and Phoebe!" Hector the fairy whispered as they disappeared in to the leaves.

Chapter 51

The Chief Scout took his fairy door management seriously. Phoebe waited whilst he popped through himself. She watched the party with a warm glow in her heart as Charlie and Elle were made welcome.

Folk helped him to a plate of food as he wheeled along and set up a table so he and Elle were in the midst of the party. After a while, Charlie's mother came along with a spaniel named Kathryn and Persephone, a west highland terrier.

With a kind voice, she told Elle it was her break time and she was free to play with the girls for a little while and do some 'dog stuff'. She was here for Charlie and there were plenty of people around.

Cautiously, as if scared she would lose him, she went off to play around the lake.

'Our time is now Paddy, hurry up' she thought. A burp behind her alerted her to his return.

"Doughnut?" he said, holding out a sugar-coated treat. She rolled her eyes. She never ate on duty.

"Paddy, Elle is on a break, our time is now...look she's there playing. We should move in".

He looked over and knew she was right. They would never have a better opportunity. He had checked and everything was in place. Winny had been asked to get Bentz to the Welcome Room but not to tell him anything in case, just to chat to Carmen and Zena at the desk. A good, diligent scout he had done just that.

"No time to lose Feebs. You talk to Elle and I shall get Bentz".

He barked loud and firm at the fairy door as Phoebe scampered over to Elle and tapped her on the shoulder.

There was no doubt when she turned around, it was like looking straight in to Bentz' beautiful eyes.

"Elle? Don't be afraid. Do the words 'Bentley Downpayment' mean anything to you?"

Elle stumbled dizzily, holding on to a wrought iron lamppost.

"Yes, yes, my Bentley, my lost boy, my treasure..." her eyes filled up with tears as she fell to the ground.

"Elle, he's safe, he's well and..." she paused as she heard two big burps behind her, "he's over there by that tree!"

"MOTHER!" squealed Bentz as he ran towards her, paws outstretched.

"BENTLEY, MY DARLING BOY!" yelped Elle as she ran towards him.

They held each other tight and cried in to each other's fur, reunited at last.

Chapter 52

Sitting on the velvet, cushion-laden sofa in the Welcome Room, Alice snuggled in to Coffee, taking comfort from the freshly laundered smell of the Queen's soft, woollen cardigan. Enveloped by her other paw, Winny sat bolt upright barely blinking, his eyes fixed on the fairy door wall.

King Bailey paced around the circular desk, first clockwise and then anti-clockwise.

Stan, Maisie and Beth sat on the desk, swinging their back paws and waiting. Hoping. Sighing.

A small crowd had started to assemble as word got out around the Kingdom.

"BURP."

"BURP."

"BURP. Pardon".

They had returned from Sark! Alice and Winny rushed through to Bentz' side and flung their paws around him.

"Was it really her? Was it?" Stanley asked, jumping down from the bench nervously.

"It was Stan, Bentz and his mother have held each other for the first time since we found him and his sisters all those dog years ago! The 'Lemonade Mission' is victorious!"

Applause broke out in the crowd, furs danced and high fived at another successful mission.

"Shusssshhhhh!" shouted Maisie as she noticed Bentz had gone a funny shade of green and unsteady on his paws, "Queen Coffee help Bentz is ill".

The Queen rushed forward and felt his forehead, stroking his cheek.

"He's fine Maisie, but you were right to holler. It's just been a lot to take in. Beth would you run through for a glass of chilled water and Stanley, please can you carry him through so we can hear all about the wonderful Lemonade Mission, learn about our new friend Elle and all sit down with some milkshakes to celebrate".

She straightened Bentz' top knot and led everyone through to the café with a happy, smiling King Bailey.

Everything had gone to plan, better than plan even!

Chapter 53

Sitting in the café with a banana milkshake and some caramel cookies, flanked by his best friend Winny and his girlfriend Alice, Bentz regained his composure and, most importantly, his smile.

His bar and café colleagues gathered around, eager to hear what had happened since Winny had run in and grabbed him earlier. Rumour had it that he was going to meet his mother, but they wanted to hear it from him.

Bentz took a deep breath.

"I found Mother!"

Cheers erupted all around him, this was the best news they could wish for. He had always believed she was alive and every shift he had asked whether any new tzus had arrived in Tzu Kingdom looking for their children. The response had always been 'no' and every time they had marked the sadness in his face.

"She is even more beautiful than I remember. Her fur is long, flowing and glossy now, her eyes are bright and sparkling and she has a plume of glory. She is quite the tiny one, I tower above her, don't I Paddy?"

Paddy nodded happily and began to fill in the back story, as he paced around the table.

"We began working on this because Bentz was so sure she was alive and so was young Beth. We started a mission with Stan, Maisie and Winny. Alice and Mac joined in along the way. We named it the 'Lemonade Mission' as we had to keep it secret, in case we weren't successful. First of all, we did our research..."

"That's right," Maisie chipped in, taking over from Paddy pacing in circles, "we looked in 'WOOF!' magazine and we saw a tzu that had been rescued and we had a hunch. She was in Kent, not too far from Wolfgang Waters and when we looked at the photo...the eyes...we were convinced...it was like looking in Bentz' eyes...we had the rescue too...Battersea Brands Hatch..."

"...so we had to get a plan together," Alice continued, rising from her seat and delicately tip pawing around the room, "one that put no tzu at risk and we called in Millie and Bella who had been homed from there...they gave us all the geo-intel we needed and, capitalising on my secret classified rescuer contacts in the area, we got the information we desired..."

Winny continued.

"This is where we called in Mac to help too. We needed experienced furs to plan the final plan and, with sandwiches and doughnuts to paw, we began to finalise the 'Lemonade Mission' with several library books borrowed to make sure we had all our ducks in a row..."

Stanley jumped up.

"...and at no time was any tzu at risk and we certainly did not break in to the rescue centre, hacking in to their computer did not even come up in conversation, we did not nearly get one of us caught nor did we run after any pairs of ear muffs...no we did not. But what we did find is exactly where Elle was and what she was up to..."

Mac sniggered and continued the walk of the story teller.

"So, we established the situation. Elle had been rescued by a big dog called Maggie, spent three nights in hospital on a drip. She was bathed, clipped and nursed back to health. Thankfully, none the worse for her experience...she is one of the lucky ones..."

"...and this is the best bit," Beth continued, once Stanley had picked her up so everyone could see her, "she trained as an assistance dog so she could help a boy called Charlie, a sitting down boy with wheels on an island called Sark, where Bentz hugged her again today".

Queen Coffee clapped her paws.

"This is all so wonderful. the 'Lemonade Mission' is a triumph. A covert operation conducted in such exemplary fashion with no unnecessary risks taken! Well done!" She smiled proudly.

Paddy and Stanley looked at each other, a little red in their faces, and shuffled their paws on the ground.

"Bravo!" added King Bailey. "Phoebe, why don't you tell us what happened today?"

Phoebe smiled at Paddy.

"We had the best day; Sark is such a beautiful island. They don't have many active fairy doors so we had to go from Little Sark to the main part of the island. We breathed in the freshest air, we soaked up the brightest sunshine, watched stunning waves and fluttering butterflies. We ran across the bridge and found Elle and her family. The fairies re-established an ancient fairy door and I spoke to a rather shocked but delighted Elle whilst Paddy got Bentz and well...I think the rest of the story belongs to him..."

Chapter 54

Bentz' eyes sparkled as he began his story.

He told his friends how he was serving up Churro Towers to a family group in the café when Winny ran in and tugged on his apron. He trusted his friend and followed him to the Welcome Room where Paddy was waiting.

Paddy took his paws and explained that, after a lengthy mission, they were 99% sure that they had found his mother. She was alive and well in Sark, working as an assistance dog to a teenage boy in a wheelchair, Phoebe was with her and he was to jump through the fairy door wall to meet her once again.

He had stumbled a little, but quickly rallied, brave as a lion and ready to see his beloved mother once again. Somewhere inside, he knew this day would come.

They arrived in Sark with a burp to find Phoebe with her paw around a small, tearful tzu. It was her. Bentz ran in to her outstretched paws. He cried and cried in to her fur, he never wanted her to let him go ever again. He had wished for this moment since the bad men took her away and he promised he would take care of his sisters.

After a while, they sat at the back of the enormous tree that housed the ancient fairy door. They cuddled in close as they talked away, there were only a few moments to be had before Elle had to return.

Bentz told his mother that he was rescued by a crack Tzu Kingdom team with his four sisters and that all five of them had happy homes across the world. She gasped as she learned about Tzu Kingdom and how they were nursed back to health in a magical place and wiped a tear to know that they were so scared at first but smiled to hear how the tzus never gave up and tended them with patience until they gained their confidence. He promised that she would soon be reunited with her daughters too, he knew King Bailey and Queen Coffee would see to that.

Elle painted a picture of her escape. She had indeed been dumped in a forest in a sealed cardboard box, but she fought her way out with her teeth and claws. She walked for miles until she found a friendly dog called Maggie who had barked to attract her kind human family's attention at which point, Elle finally collapsed.

Through a haze, she was aware of Maggie's human father picking her up and wrapping her in his fleece. She felt the warmth envelop her as they ran speedily through the trees and into a car, with her new friend's human mother and siblings in hot pursuit. They raced to their own vet where she was admitted as an emergency.

She remembered them talking to the nice people in blue pyjamas, saying that they had to try to save her and that they would pay for her treatment. They were lucky they said, they could help, and the children stroked Elle and wished her better. They were sad though, because they were not able to take another dog in to their home just now. But, they said, they would take her to Battersea Brands Hatch and find just the right family for her. All she had to do was get better.

A week later, after a few baths, a furcut and some hearty meals, they all climbed in the car again and took her to the rescue centre. The children cried a little, as did Maggie as they said their goodbyes. But this was the right and sensible thing to do to find her the perfect home where she could have individual attention. She needed calm and, Maggie's house was full of love but calm it was not!

When she arrived, a miracle happened. A family had been in touch looking for a rescue dog to be a constant companion and assistance dog to their disabled son. He was very poorly and he would not grow to be old. He needed help every day and they wondered whether Elle would be just right for him. Within a few days, she was training for her new job and, the most exciting thing, they were shortly to move to Sark for a calm and peaceful life for Charlie to live out his remaining years.

Chapter 55

"...and that's where we are now," Bentz finished.

"Well, what a wonderful story," Queen Coffee sniffed, emotionally.

"Bentz this is a big day for you and your friends will help you celebrate so no more table waiting today OK? You celebrate with milkshakes, juice and cakes and tell them all about your big adventure".

"Bentz, will Elle want to visit Tzu Kingdom?"

"Oh yes please Queen. She says she will come and see me and I can show her around. Mother has responsibilities at home of course, but she will make time for all of us. I can't wait! Winny and I can make her a cake in Tzu Bakery right?"

Winny hugged his friend and the Queen smiled.

"Bailey, we have work to do dear. Let's call Kiki and Lola and ask them if they would kindly pop through to Molly, Michelle, Ellen and Rosa and tell them their mother is waiting to meet them".

Bentz raised his paw.

"Yes little fella?" asked King Bailey.

"Oh King. May I just say thank you to the 'Lemonade Mission'. They worked so hard to reunite me with mother and my dream has come true. I must be the happiest tzu in the world right now! I also want to special thank Paddy for keeping me so calm today".

Stanley slapped Paddy on the back to congratulate him. He had grown as a tzu and in to his senior role. A few years ago,

Paddy would have been the one that needed calming and now, here he was helping the youngsters. Paddy blushed and shrugged his shoulders.

The King nodded.

"Indeed yes, well done to the 'Lemonade Mission'. Paddy, Stanley, Maisie, Beth, Winny, Alice and Mac are an example to us all and we owe them our immense gratitude. They have, over the past few months been brave, been careful and been Tzu.

"Brave as Lions!"

"BRAVE AS LIONS!" echoed the crowd as the royal couple exited the café and headed to their office.

As they left, they passed Brickie and Hiro arriving for a snack. With a burp, the brothers headed over to the gathering and caught up with Mac on the way.

"What's going on?" asked Brickie.

"Great news," Mac responded, "we have found Bentz' mother!"

Hiro's eyes lit up. "Oh, pretty Elle who lives on Sark with the sitting down boy on wheels?"

"What?" said a shocked Mac, "how did you know this? We have run a daring covert mission over months, we only just heard the story..."

"Well, I told Brickie about her months ago, when we had our Scout Tower training. He told me to keep quiet about the tzu voices in my head and called me mystic".

Brickie was startled. "Well, I thought furs would laugh at you. Oh Mac, should I have told him to keep it quiet or not, I was just protecting my brother?"

Mac stroked his beard. "Hmmm, we should keep this to the three of us, everything is all OK but, let's bear this in mind because it seems to me that Hiro has a gift".

Chapter 56

Coffee sniggered as she walked along the corridor.

"Stop it," said Bailey, "you'll start me off!"

She quickened her steps and held her pashmina up to her giggling mouth.

Bailey sniggered too. He could hardly bark code the door open when they arrived.

They both hurried through the door, slamming it behind them.

The Queen took a deep breath and looked at her husband.

"They broke in to the rescue centre and hacked the computer, didn't they?"

"Totally!" the King replied.

They both collapsed on a nearby beanbag in fits of laughter.

"Oh Coffee, those youngsters, they think we don't know? You and I have done our share of such capers in our time!"

"When we were younger, dear heart, and faster! Do you remember when we broke in to that horrid pet shop with Nancy, Otis keeping look out from Scout Tower? Pierre never suspected a thing!"

"We saved three little puppies that night - Nico, Wickett and Mallett. I don't regret it for a moment. Whatever happened, they got the right outcome. Those little lions should be proud of themselves".

They held paws and laughed on the beanbags, swinging their legs in the air and remembering the days gone by.

Chapter 57

Hotel Battenberg stood on the River Seine, majestic and opulent. It was the perfect place for the wedding of a Tzu King and his betrothed.

An historic building over seven floors and bursting with Parisian charm, the hotel was one of the best in the world and a must-visit for all celebrity dogs for, here, the canines were as welcome as their owners, if not more so.

Awaiting the Royal Party at the Canine Concierge Desk was Louis shih tzu, with his flowing blond ears and plume of glory, a dear friend of Bailey and Coffee. He had enormous responsibilities at the hotel so struggled to get to Tzu Kingdom often, but he was extremely popular with all furs when he did drop in, often with a new cocktail recipe or a pastry idea for Tzu Bakery.

Five burps in quick succession alerted Louis to his guests. Nancy first, then King Bailey, Miss Coffee, Centime and Franc. Louis hugged them all.

"Welcome to Hotel Battenberg, I am honoured to be performing the ceremony with the power invested in me as a Canine Concierge. I have arranged us a suite overlooking the Eiffel Tower...follow me..."

Louis unhooked a bunch of keys and led them to the lift. As they walked, they admired the flowers cascading down waterfalls, the lights of colour shining through the arched stained-glass windows and the chandeliers above their heads".

"What a place to live Louis, you are one lucky pup!"

"I can't disagree with you there Bailey dear pal, I have rather landed on my paws!" Louis laughed as he took an extending

wand from his inside uniform pocket and pulled it out to its full length, pressing the button for their floor.

Inside the suite was a sumptuous spread - as Nancy had been promised - with a view of the Eiffel Tower.

A four-poster big bed was too tempting, and the girls ran towards it, boinging on to it from the floor and bouncing up and down on the luxurious pillows and cushions.

"Oh Bailey, I am sorry," laughed Coffee, "are you sure I am not too silly to be your Queen?"

Bailey boinged on to the bed with them.

"More sure than ever Sweetpea! Being Royal doesn't mean being stuffy. We just have to watch who's around!"

"You're safe with us!" yelled Franc as he jumped on the bed too.

"You boing and bounce away! Housekeeping will remake the bed when we are out. But, well, there's something I need to talk to you about".

Louis looked serious.

"If any fur ever asks, you married in shadow of 'la tour Eiffel'. Oui? But I have a secret and it's a big one".

"The place where I will officiate over Coffee and Bailey taking their vows is a secret location, with a fairy door only known to a few tzus. Legend has it that Queen Sally installed it and its existence has been passed down through every Hotel Battenberg Canine Concierge that has been before me".

He beckoned them to follow him once more to the balcony where they gasped at the sight of Paris in all its beautiful glory. He pointed his paw up to the very top of the tower.

"If it suits you both, you will marry inside the Eiffel Tower. At Gustave Eiffel's apartment".

156

Chapter 58

Two hundred and seventy-six metres from the ground, Louis stepped out on to the third level of the world-famous Eiffel Tower.

Nancy jumped through after him and stood next to him as he indicated. Coffee held on to King Bailey's paw, knowing he was a little scared of heights and as brave as a lion to even agree to venture to such a height.

"I am at my bravest with your paw in mine," he had assured her, as she had excitedly jumped up and down at the thought of a sky-high wedding.

The six of them stood huddled together by the door, each letting out a little burp. Louis had instructions to impart.

"Welcome to the top of the Eiffel Tower and Gustave's own apartment, lovingly restored to its original glory in recent years. You will see Monsieur Eiffel and his friend Thomas Edison in waxwork form at the table here...Gustave loved dogs and, in fact, a photograph of one of his dogs hangs today in the 'Musée d'Orsay' here in Paris..."

The furs giggled at the pretend people in their static conversation.

"...they won't move or bother us," laughed Louis, "but the tower is open to the public and they may peer through. We need to stay on the fairy door side of the room, as so to hide, but if a human sees a wagging tail, they will just assume they are dizzy from heights and probably never mention it!"

"As I said, legend has it that Queen Sally installed this fairy door and it has only been known to selective furs, King Pierre told Franc and Centime many moons ago and I was privy to this secret as a Canine Concierge of Paris. It was foretold that, one day, its use would reveal itself and, well, when Nancy appeared earlier, I could not think of a more perfect occasion".

Coffee and Bailey smiled at each other. Maybe this was meant to be.

"As allowed in dog law, a concierge can officiate a wedding and it is my privilege to do so, for my dear friends. Coffee, you look stunning in your gown of lace and Bailey, you always suited a bowtie!"

"So, if the bride and groom could hold paws just here...Nancy, you just here and Franc and Centime, to this side. I think we are ready to marry!"

Chapter 59

Coffee, I would take the stars
Out of the sky for you
Stop the rain from falling
If you asked me to
I'd do anything for you
Your wish is my command
I could climb a mountain when
Your paw is in my paw

Bailey, to me you are
My funny clown
Who picks me up
Each time I'm down
You bring out
The best in me
So, let's together
Always be
Paw in Paw

The couple's vows had everyone in tears and Louis made a proclamation.

"I now pronounce you husband and wife as well as King and Queen of Tzu Kingdom".

King Bailey pulled his beautiful Queen Coffee close to him and gave her a kiss. She smiled and stroked his beard.

"I love you!" they said to each other.

Nancy shed a tear and ran to hug them both. Franc and Centime followed and joined in the special moment.

"Well, it's time to head back to Hotel Battenberg," Louis announced as he jumped back through the fairy door to put the finishing touches to their wedding breakfast.

* * *

Back at Hotel Battenberg, two little tzus were waiting in anticipation to meet King Bailey and his new wife, Queen Coffee. They waited in reception hiding behind a velvet covered chair with paws full of confetti.

Louis saw them as he came in and waved. It was strange, he had no dogs arriving today and he would certainly have remembered if two shih tzus were due. He made a note in his head to come back and investigate as soon as the wedding party was underway. It might have been a late booking, he pondered.

The smallest tzu waved back, only to be grabbed around the waist and pulled behind the chair by her travelling companion.

"Smarty! We are supposed to be keeping a low profile!"

"Oh, but Professor did you see his fur! So shiny and so handsome!"

"There'll be time enough for that young lady...and I think the sooner I drop you off with your new family the better!" giggled the older girl.

A shrill of laughter caught their attention.

"They're here!" squealed the little one. "Oh my, Queen Coffee is beautiful, look at her ears..."

Walking towards them were five laughing shih tzus, a small black and white tzu in a bow tie was carrying a slightly larger coffee and caramel tzu in his paws, her ears flowing behind her whilst she playfully bounced her flowers off his head, and jokingly pleading with him to put her down, even though she was clearly enjoying it.

"We'll take the stairs, King and Queen, you two take the lift so Bailey can carry you over a threshold," laughed a white tzu, running off with two friends and leaving them behind.

"I am a modern fur Mr Bailey, unpaw me! Your Queen demands it," she sniggered.

"Oh, perhaps you want to carry me instead?" he spluttered, laughing so much he had to put her down to clutch his sides.

They fell to the floor full of mirth, then looked at each other seriously.

"Everything we do my sweet, we do as a team, with love, trust and support. We are equal partners, in marriage and as the rulers of Tzu Kingdom".

Queen Coffee nodded, it was just as they had agreed, and it was right.

"Let's go over the threshold paw-in-paw, start as we mean to go on".

They stood and turned towards the ornate lift to find two little tzus stood in front of them.

"CONGRATULATIONS!" they bellowed, throwing confetti and glitter over the pair before running off in to the maze of chairs and out into the night along the River Seine and jumping through a fairy door on the river.

"Who were they and where did they go?" the Queen asked, looking around eagerly.

Coffee and Bailey hadn't seen them leave the hotel or jump through the fairy door by the front entrance.

"They must be hotel guests; I suppose they're playing around the chairs like silly lemons! We'll mention it to Louis when we get upstairs," Bailey replied as they stepped in to the lift.

Chapter 60

The 'Jewel Eye Crown' of the Tzu Queens had been crafted for Queen Sally in 1947, at the insistence of the fairies. The first queen only thought she was standing in for King Wolfgang until his return and, therefore, it was not until two years after his disappearance that she acquiesced and agreed that they could craft a crown for her. On one condition. Hers would complement the King's crown and would always look for him. The fairies set a pair of jewel eyes in the reverse of the crown, watching and waiting for King Wolfgang's return.

He never again took to the throne and, once Sally closed her eyes for the last time and Romeo became King, the crown was stored in the vault, beneath the library. King Romeo inherited Wolfgang's crown and the Queen's crown was not seen again until 1985 at Queen Gypsophilia's coronation. It had been stored away once more between 1991 and 1999 and again, wrapped in a silken cloth, since 2004.

Earlier this evening, Nancy had bark coded her way in to the vault, retrieved the Jewel Eye Crown, running it through to Hotel Battenberg where, back in the suite Louis had reserved for the wedding party, King Bailey placed the fur-loom on the head of his new wife.

New Queen Coffee was honoured, she hadn't given a moment's thought to a crown, more concerned was she with supporting her beloved Bailey, Tzu Kingdom and its furs but, she had to admit, she loved it.

Vanity had no place in Coffee's heart or mind yet, as she looked in the mirror, she liked what she saw. She thought of Sally, Gypsophilia and Mirabelle, the Queens before her, and felt humbled. The Jewel Eye Crown was beautiful, and it served to remind her of her responsibilities, shared with Bailey, but her responsibilities nonetheless.

"I can't imagine the crown ever looking more regal or beautiful," Bailey said as she joined him back on the velvet sofa, walking elegantly as she tried to keep it on. Overnight, she knew it would magically make itself fit to her head perfectly.

"Plus," she giggled, "I suppose I really do have eyes in the back of my head now!"

"Well, I didn't like to say but you do always seem to know what is going on...I think the eyes have found their perfect place," laughed Nancy. She burped, it turned into a yawn and then she slunk back in her armchair, snoring.

Everyone was exhausted from dancing and full of sumptuous buffet food. Louis kept apologising for only laying on a small spread at short notice but there was so much left over, and he thought maybe he had over-catered after all. Coffee looked over at the table.

"Bailey, we can't let all this food be thrown away. It's a waste and there must be furs in need that would be glad of a meal. Maybe we can drop it through to them or distribute it before we leave for our homes?"

Centime piped up. "Queen Coffee, Maman collects donations for zee refuge pour chiens. Perhaps you would like to leave them at our apartment building for her to deliver at zee weekend?"

"Excellent idea!" agreed Franc, "Louis and I will parcel it all up in boxes and we shall deliver it to the door. Would you like to join us King and Queen? See a little of Paris?"

"We would love to!" they said together, jumping up ready to depart. They left their crowns on the sofa and soon headed off to the suburbs where Franc and Centime lived in a luxury apartment. They would call back for them shortly, as well as a slightly tired and emotional Nancy, on their way home via Tzu Kingdom. First, they would take Nancy to Swansea, then off to Coffee's home in Ontario and finally to Bailey's modest home in Essex.

"Louis, please keep a watch over Nancy, we will return as soon as we are able," Bailey asked his good friend.

"Oh, and Louis," Coffee interjected as she buttoned her coat, "we saw two lovely young lady tzus in reception earlier. We didn't recognise them at all. Are they guests here?"

Louis looked a little flushed.

"Oh yes, thank you for reminding me Queen Coffee. New guests that arrived late this evening. I shall visit them in the morning and welcome them formally".

"Thank you Louis, it's my job to look after all the tzus now, especially the girls. I imagine I will meet them in time".

Louis nodded. "I have a feeling you will Queen, in time, in time".

Feeling assured, the Royal couple left on their first formal engagement together, following Franc and Centime through the fairy door to their apartment, laden with boxes of treats for the shelter dogs of Paris.

Tomorrow, they would announce to the Kingdom that it now had a King and Queen to rule equally.

Once they had jumped, Nancy opened an eye.

"You saw them Louis? Really? Were they OK? Is it all going to plan?"

Louis smiled and flopped on the chair with Nancy.

"Yes, they were weaving in and out of the chairs in reception. I didn't understand at first and then I remembered. When I got up here, I looked out of the window and I saw them jump through the fairy door, just as foretold".

Chapter 61

"What's the craic?" asked Paddy as he joined Stanley and Maisie on the picnic blanket under the oak tree. They were having a breath of fresh air before they started dress rehearsals for the big event of the year – Coffee and Bailey's Marriage Renewal.

"Maisie has big news Pads," his best friend answered, "and even I don't know what it is! She says she wants us to be the first to hear and before we get busy later".

Maisie was beaming from ear to ear and she poured the boys a juice for her huge announcement. With a deep breath, she began her story.

"Well boys, something has happened at my house in tribute to my much-missed big sister Nancy."

"You know of course that Mummy Megan built the Grandpops Annexe for Grandpops Ifan to live out his days with Nancy and of course, it has stood empty for many months now. But, as you know with my Mummy, there was always a plan".

"Go on..." nodded Paddy.

"We had the builders back and it's been altered, redecorated and we are now all set. Shortly, we will be opening 'Nancy Noodle House' – a home for older shih tzus and small dogs that have been abandoned in their old age or, perhaps, left alone when their humans could no longer care for them. Well, they will live with us now and we will either find them a forever foster home or just keep them there in Grandpops place for always".

Stanley was happy, but a little confused.

"So, how will they cope living on their own Maisie? Who will put the football on the TV and give them their dinner and play fetch with them?"

Maisie smiled.

"They won't be on their own Stan. Mummy is taking on staff! That's what has changed. The annexe is quite big and there are two lovely bedrooms now, each with a sparkling white bathroom and windows over the garden. We will employ two young people to live in and look after them round the clock, well in shifts. We have already got one young lady moving in at the weekend – she is called Sabrina and I think she's enchanted – even though I hear she comes from a non-enchanted family. That's why I needed to tell you today, in case you saw a new person and wondered who she was!"

The boys were so happy. This was the perfect tribute to Nancy. Stanley didn't let on that he had seen it in a magazine, but he sure was proud of his girlfriend.

"Will you tell King Bailey and Queen Coffee?" Paddy asked.

She nodded. She had an appointment with the Queen in just a while.

"It's perfect," Stanley mused, his eyes lighting up as a thought popped in to his head. "Do you think this is anything to do with you and Beth mysteriously turning up there? Maybe it put the idea in your mummy's bonce?"

Her eyes twinkled and she giggled. Stanley gasped, realising that the scout plans that he had been part of during his tenure had led to something beyond his wild dreams – a safe house for tzus-less-fortunate and a chance for them to live the winters of their lives in happiness and comfort, with people that loved them.

Paddy wiped a tear from his fur. It was just the lift he needed as Chief Scout. He realised how crucial his role was and the difference it made to tzus like King Bailey, deserted at the time they need love most.

"So, we have a safe place to drop any older tzus we rescue now. A real safe place, with no question that they will be loved until they close their eyes for the last time". Overwhelmed, he burst in to tears of happiness and Stanley and Maisie ran to hug him close.

"I'm OK, I'm OK," cried Paddy, his shoulders shaking, "it's just that most people want puppies but humans like your mummy and human sisters are special, they love the old ones, the broken ones and the troubled ones. You truly belong to an enchanted family".

Stanley tickled his tummy and made him laugh. "Why don't we all go and tell Bailey and Coffee? Is that OK Maisie?"

"Of course, it is! Come on boys, keep up!" hollered Maisie as she ran to the Royal Chamber Patio with her friends in hot pursuit, knowing that Paddy was right. Beth and she had, indeed, landed on their paws.

Chapter 62

Luna, singer of the Kingdom band Tzu Aroo, waved at Mac when she got to the top of the balcony that had been constructed on the stage in the Party Room. With the roving mike in her paw, she was ready for the sound check.

Mac waved back. He wanted everything to be perfect at the Tzu Renew celebration party. Luna had already tested the floor, all four corners of the stage and every step on the way up to the bridge area from where Mac would narrate the show.

'The History of Tzu Kingdom' was going to be nothing short of amazing.

"One, two, one two," Luna chanted. Mac gave her a thumbs up and she ran up the stairs. "One, two, one two," again.

"Luna, could you sing something with lots of high notes in it so I can check me trebles," Mac hollered, "start up top on the bridge, walk along, up the back where the big finish will start from and down to the front again please...be careful on the steps..."

Luna had a stunning voice. Now settled in her new home and happy beyond her wildest dreams, she was a kind and generous friend to every tzu. Tonight was a big night for her. She would open the show as Mac compered.

"Why do fairies suddenly appear
Every time you are near?
Just like me, they long to be
Close to you

"Why do stars fall down from the sky
Every time you paw step by?
Just like me, they long to be
Close to you

169

"On the day that you were born the angels got together
And decided to create a dream come true
So they sprinkled moon dust in your fur of gold and starlight
in your eyes of blue".

Mac smiled. It was sounding good. They were ready for the dress rehearsal now.

A slam of door and Paddy and Stanley crashed through to the Party Room, in full costume, followed by Lola and Kiki, just the same. They looked amazing and they twirled around.

"What do you think?" asked Lola.

"Amazing," said Mac, "how is everyone doing?"

"They're nearly all ready," Kiki assured him. Mac had pulled the show together almost single-pawed and he was nervous as he set up the projector that would provide an inspirational end piece slide show about the story of Bailey and Coffee so far.

"You know, they're going to love it!" Paddy assured him, playfully digging him in his tummy.

"Oh well, I sure did!" Stanley agreed, pinching his nose and making him sneeze.

But then another fur crashed in through the door, it was Bonnie, looking flushed and out of breath after running from Scout Tower.

"Mayday! Mayday! Emergency situation. The young girls from fairy door Dorset 1877 – Millie and Bella – they've been dognapped".

Chapter 63

The car hurtled along the motorway at dangerous speed. Bella felt sick and looked at Millie with tears in her eyes. The eldest by three minutes, Millie had never shirked her responsibility and reached out for her sister's paw to reassure her.

It had all happened so quickly.

Mummy had put them in the car with their seatbelts on and then remembered she had a birthday card to post. They watched her jump out of the car, unlock the door and trot in to the kitchen after doing the thing that she had been told off about by Daddy more times than they cared to remember – leaving her keys in the door.

Twice since they lived with her, he had returned home from work to find them still hanging there, waiting for a passing thief to take their things. Mummy would sigh and roll her eyes, saying that's not going to happen. The tzus didn't dare tell him how many times she remembered the keys before he arrived.

But now it had, indeed, happened. In that few seconds two bad men stole the keys, jumped in the car and drove them away. But not just them, their three-year-old human brother Johan too. Millie had to do some fast thinking. With Bella feeling queasy and Johan dozing off, blissfully unaware of their predicament, she had to save them. It was time to get noticed.

"BARK BARK BARK BARK BARK BARK," Millie barked.

"There's dogs in the back," said the man in the passenger seat.

"Ok, we'll turn off and dump them, there's an old industrial estate up here, we'll chuck them in one of the buildings," said the man at the wheel.

"We can't do that," his partner in crime replied, "what would happen to them".

The driver man shrugged.

"No way. My Nan's got a little dog like these ones – shih tzus – they are lovely dogs and they'll never survive alone. I just wanted to make some quick money; I don't want to break anyone's hearts".

"Oh, for goodness sake, they're just dogs, it's not like they're children or anything important".

The passenger man gasped. "How DARE you!" he exclaimed, turning around to stroke Bella, who growled at him.

"Hey little one, don't be scared. I won't hurt you," he said, emphasising the 'I'. "Oh no," he shouted, turning back to the front and turning crimson red".

"What?" the driver man sighed.

"There's a little boy in the back too".

Chapter 64

Millie was scared now. All she had to put her faith in was the passenger man and she didn't like him much at all. Mummy must be frantic – her three children out of her sight.

Bella moved in close and whispered to her.

"If we bark some more, maybe Scout Tower might hear us and send a rescue team?"

"Brilliant idea Bella! Let's bark!"

"BARK BARK BARK BARK BARK BARK".

"I CAN'T HEAR MYSELF THINK!" said the driver man. "STOP BARKING!" he screamed. But the girls carried on and, in to the mix, Johan woke up and started crying. "One more bark and I am turning those two creatures out on the road and leaving them to fend for themselves".

"No, you can't do that. Let's dump the car with them all in it. The police will be looking for us now, what with the baby and all..." passenger man suggested.

He wasn't so bad, he had just got caught up with the wrong people, but he wasn't going to let anyone hurt a dog. He looked at Millie again and she knew this was her opportunity to help him too. They looked in to each other's eyes. She looked down at the floor where Mummy's handbag lay, with contents that were bound to placate the driver man.

"There's cash in here," said passenger man, pulling an envelope out and counting it quickly. "It's over a grand – that'll do for a hard day's work won't it? There's a good phone but let's leave it, in case they trace us". He winked at Millie and she winked back. That was one lovely week in a cottage that they wouldn't be having now, but it was worth it. She looked at him earnestly and wondered, was he enchanted once? He was only young; he didn't need a life of crime. Maybe this had all happened for a reason, she could only hope.

They arrived at the disused site, full of crumbling buildings with smashed windows, fading signage and notices warning people to keep out. The car stopped behind a former car repair shop where the men jumped out.

"Let's run," said the driver man, scarpering over the hill without even looking back for his friend.

Passenger man stopped for a second, he opened all the windows to make sure Millie, Bella and Johan had air. He stroked both tzus and they wagged their tails.

"Bye little doggies, I hope you'll be found soon," he said, tearfully as he ran over the hill.

Chapter 65

It was cold with the windows down and Millie and Bella huddled together with Johan for warmth.

They were all in their seatbelts, safe, but anchored. Johan was calling for his Mummy and they quietly consoled him.

Above them, they could hear sirens and they knew they were being sought, but would anyone think to look here?

Suddenly, a pair of paws appeared on the window and, standing on Kiki's shoulders, Lola appeared.

"Thank dog!" she exclaimed!

Johan laughed. "Hi pretty doggy, hi pretty doggy!" he said, excited to see another tzu, trusting he was safe.

"Hi Johan, Millie, Bella," ok I'm coming in she said, climbing through the half open window and checking them over.

She opened the door to let Kiki in, followed by Comforter Otto with a revival kit in his back pack.

"Sip this water," he said as he passed them a flask of water, concerned, as he checked them over. Kiki pulled a blanket out of his bag and tucked it in around them all.

"You seem OK, no harm done I don't think," Otto confirmed, "Scout Tower was watching so we knew where you were. Thankfully there's a fairy door just at the end of the estate. I think this used to be countryside once..." he said sadly.

"Scout Tower. Fairy Door. Countryside..." repeated Johan, making shy Otto smile. It seemed he was an enchanted child.

Lola moved things on.

"We have to get some humans here to find you. They'll never do it on their own, this place is abandoned, and they don't have the magic telescopes like the scouts do".

"I have an idea," Millie offered, "they left Mummy's phone in her bag, they just took the money. They said that it might be able to be traced".

Kiki delved straight in to find it. She rolled her eyes. "Flat as a pancake, typical, just like mine!"

"What would they do without us?" Lola sighed, unzipping a pocket and pulling out an all-purpose phone charger. She jumped through to the front seat, with both paws she turned the keys in the ignition and plugged the phone in to charge.

Stroking the captive girls' ears, Kiki explained that as soon as the phone had a little charge, they would call the emergency people who would trace the call. The rescue team would watch from a distance until they were safe and then jump back through to Tzu Kingdom. A scout would visit them tomorrow to follow up and close the mission down.

"Thank you so much," Bella sniffled.

"We always have you covered in Tzu Kingdom," Kiki assured them.

Lola looked through the seats in to the back.

"Ok, I have 20%, I'm calling 999. When I do bark and cry, they'll be here in no time okay?"

With a firm paw, she pressed the 9 key three times and the green key.

"Okay run!" said Kiki as they jumped out of the car and hid behind a dead tree.

Sure enough, within a few minutes they could hear sirens and they got louder and louder until they all had to cover their ears with their paws. A police car door flung open and their Mummy jumped out and ran to the car, scooping her three babies up in her arms and sobbing.

* * *

The team arrived back in the Welcomer Room and high-pawed each other. It was strange, usually there would be a crowd gathering but the dress rehearsal was underway and the Royal couple had agreed to keep away whilst it went on, so as not to spoil anything.

Zena and Carmen welcomed them back, congratulating them on a mission accomplished.

Otto looked pensive.

"Lola, Kiki, how are they going to explain how the phone got out of the handbag, plugged itself in and dialled the police all whilst Johan, Millie and Bella where in the back in their seatbelts. I mean, won't that all feel a bit strange?"

The girls giggled.

"Yeah, so not our problem," Lola laughed swishing her tail.

Chapter 66

Something amazing and more than a little incredible had arrived in the Party Room. The gathered tzus were woofless. Tzu Bakery had excelled itself for the Royal couple's special day.

Luna found her voice.

"Jiro, where did you get your inspiration from?"

The baker tzu smiled proudly as he slowly spun the cake around on its stand. It stood tall, at least six times the height of the tallest tzu.

"Well, I'm glad you asked me that," he glowed, "perhaps I can take you through the layers?"

His friends nodded and formed a circle around him.

The first layer was a classic sponge, containing high quality sausages, celebrating the favoured dish of all Tzu Kingdom parties. A selection of dips including gravy, marrowbone sauce, mustard and ketchup was offered on the side.

Balanced on top was the tier entitled 'cheeses of the world' that would demonstrate Coffee and Bailey's international diplomatic work with other dog worlds.

Atop the cheese was the pork pie and quiche layer, to show the fun that they had at parties and the mastery of Tzu Bakery.

Mackerel fillets were the next layer, Coffee's favourite dish for keeping shiny fur and bright eyes.

Above the fish course, the desserts began, with a nutritious cake packed full of fruit in tribute to the magic orchard.

A Battenberg Cake, in recognition of their original wedding, nestled above, resplendent in pink and yellow and covered in tasty marzipan.

"...and that's where we have gotten to until tomorrow," Jiro finished, "when I will add the tutti frutti ice cream block, the whipped cream and then, finally, the sugar crafted Eiffel Tower and tiny wedding couple!

Rapturous applause broke out. Stanley cleared his throat as Paddy rapped on the floor asking for quiet.

"Jiro and Tzu Bakery," he began nervously, "I think I speak for everyone when I say that we are hugely impressed and fortunate in the extreme to have you as part of Tzu Kingdom. The cake is going to be an amazing surprise for the King and Queen. Thank you on behalf of us all".

Jiro blushed.

"It's a team effort DCS Stanley, I had a lot of new bakers to help me this year and I think the future of Tzu Bakery is assured!"

"Keep those doughnuts coming!" Paddy exclaimed, to everyone's laughter.

Chapter 67

Tzu Renew Day was here and, out in the Tzu Kingdom gardens, hundreds of tzus sat in a circle, nervously anticipating the arrival of King Bailey and Queen Coffee to renew their vows.

A stunning arch of gold and white flowers stood twinkling in the sunset. This was the stage for the renewal, and it was all set.

It was to be a simple ceremony, with just the two of them addressing each other but, this time with all their friends in attendance, their vows would be heard across the Kingdom and a portrait would appear in Tzu Gallery for future generations to celebrate the love of the King and Queen.

A tzu harpist played gentle music as the excited crowds gathered. Stanley and Maisie sat at the front with Paddy and Phoebe, all in their finest outfits. The boys wore their best suits from the state occasion when King Wolfgang had visited. Maisie wore a floral maxi dress with fur fascinator and Phoebe, a blue jumpsuit set off with a large floppy hat. They were at the front with a space ready for Beth, who was to be flower girl. She was to join them once her official duties had been completed.

Excitement spread across the crowd and they rose to their paws as the patio doors opened and the harpist played an up-tempo arrangement for their arrival.

Beth appeared, beaming from ear to ear with a basket of white petals and began her journey to the stage. King Bailey followed, resplendent in his tuxedo, turning to take Queen Coffee's paw in his as they stepped through on to their private patio and walked, happily, paw in paw to renew their vows.

There wasn't a dry eye in the house as the assembled tzus witnessed their rulers follow the path that took them, following Beth's petal trail, in a full circle around the centre arch so everyone could see them and admire Coffee's golden gown. In recognition of the occasion, both wore their crowns, and they twinkled in the sunlight.

Maisie nudged Stanley. "Did Coffee's crown just wink at me?" she asked him, sure that she had seen one of the jewel eyes in the back of the Queen's crown seek her out. Stanley giggled, "probably just a trick of the light!"

Bailey and Coffee arrived at the centre and waved at their flock. Coffee passed her bouquet to Beth. The little girl curtsied and took her seat between Maisie and Phoebe.

The King turned to the congregation, cleared his throat and spoke.

"Tzus, our beloved friends, thank you for gathering today to join us for 'Tzus Renew' where Queen Coffee and I will once again make our lifelong commitment to each other.

"As you know, our original betrothal took place in the shadow of the Eiffel Tower and it was the most amazing day of my life to be proposed to by the girl with the most beautiful ears and the kindest heart and, finally, after she turned me down twice, to marry her and make her my wife and your Queen.

"I arrived in Tzu Kingdom as a matted, grubby stray on the brink of closing my eyes for the last time yet, thanks to love, I am the happy dog that stands before you today, King of Tzu Kingdom and husband of the amazing Queen Coffee.

"Many say that the legend foretells that we are chosen ones but, I am the lucky one I feel and, this beautiful fur is my chosen one and the love of my life".

The audience awed and sniffed. Coffee recovered her composure and continued.

"My dear sweet friends, I love that so many of you have joined us today for this special occasion. You will know that this is partly in tribute to my dear friend Nancy and this makes me reflect as I look around. I had some wonderful times with Nancy, but I see you today looking at us up here, I think of the wonderful times I have had with so many of you in my days in Scout Tower as well as my time as Queen. I am thankful to Sirius Star in the sky for everything in my life, for every one of you, but especially for my dear, handsome Mr Bailey Sirius Star whom I loved from the moment I laid my eyes upon him".

Handkerchiefs changed paws and friends held each other tight as they felt the love between the royal couple.

They took each other's paws and repeated the vows they had made years before, in Paris.

Coffee, I would take the stars
Out of the sky for you
Stop the rain from falling
If you asked me to
I'd do anything for you
Your wish is my command
I could climb a mountain when
Your paw is in my paw

Bailey, to me you are
My funny clown
Who picks me up
Each time I'm down
You bring out
The best in me
So, let's together
Always be
Paw in Paw

Chapter 68

"Come through, come through. Take your seats. There are canapes to share. Yes, please take your drinks through. There's champagne, juice and milk shakes on the bar..." said the bar keep tzus as they waived the congregation through to the Party Room.

The excitement buzzed in the air and friends kissed and hugged as they sat down for the show.

It was quite an extravaganza with a beautiful stage setting. The bridge had been completed with twin staircases constructed down to the main stage. An old-fashioned projector was set at the back of the room, ready to run reel-to-reel and they wondered what for as they shared the canapes.

Mac and Luna peeked out nervously from behind the curtain and then turned to smile at the assembled cast, all awaiting their cue.

"Ok team, it's almost time" said Mac, checking his roving microphone was switched off for now. He was to narrate the show he had directed, and he was trying to remain calm. Rehearsals had gone well and now, in their costumes, everything was ready. He in a velvet jacket and Luna, ready to start the show as a trapped fairy, felt quite the part in her fluttering wings.

There were two extremely special guests still to arrive and they would be led to their seats by the grand-dames of the Comforter Wing, Mabel and Myrtle.

"They're at the doors!" shrieked Maisie, excited to see them again in their wedding outfits. In they came, smiling and laughing with their good friends and walked through to the front where an elegant sofa awaited, waving to everyone on the way.

The royal couple sat as Mable and Myrtle hushed the audience.

It was time for the show.

Chapter 69

Mac, atop the bridge, barked in to his microphone.

"Welcome to the story of Tzu Kingdom!" he announced as the band began to play.

Centre stage, an ensemble of tzus danced and played to the music of Tzu Aroo. They performed a 'cha cha cha' – Queen Coffee's favourite -and shimmied around – King Bailey style - to much laughter. Sound effects brought bird song to a bright, sunlit stage.

Suddenly, the stage darkened, the bird song stopped and storm noises crashed around the stage. At this point, the dance troop screamed and ran off stage.

"Help! Help!" came a tiny voice stage left. A spotlight illuminated to reveal fairy Luna trapped by her wings in a net, following a violent storm.

"Oh my," Mac narrated, "look at the fairy trapped by her wings down at the riverside, she is in mortal peril. Who on earth will save her?"

A gong sounded and echoed throughout the room. Next to Mac appeared a black and white tzu, dressed in a long oriental coat.

The spotlight revealed it was Hiro.

"I will save you," he barked, heroically, as he ran down the steps, with Mac helping the story to unfold.

"Why, it's a brave chap called Leo and he's leading a delegation of tzus down to the river to save the fairies".

The ensemble was back, and they gathered around Luna the fairy. Within seconds she was free, spinning around with her wings fluttering free. She ran around hugging and thanking them and then to the gasps of the crowd she took off in to the sky, landing next to Mac on the bridge, powered by a little Christmas sprinkle magic!

Luna loved being the fairy and she danced around with a spring in her paws, flying along the bridge, around Mac and doing air cartwheels. Then she stopped.

"Fairy Luna, whatever is wrong?" he enquired, noticing her face of worry.

"We fairies must thank those little dogs," she sung sweetly, flying down the stairs and arriving centre stage. She took Leo/Hiro's paw and danced some more, waltzing around the room. As they danced, lights appeared around them in the shape of tiny doors. On her departure, Luna twirled and covered him in fairy dust.

"That's the enchantment spell," the narrator informed the audience, "shih tzus can now shrink down and jump through the fairy doors!"

The troop, led by Leo/Hiro danced in and out of the doors, partying away. They lined up in the centre of the circle and then stepped aside to reveal a throne, where Leo/Hiro sat wearing a crown.

"Tzu Kingdom has been created!" yelled Mac, to a cheering crowd.

The ensemble held him aloft and finally danced through to the back of the stage as it went momentarily dark and quiet.

'Ding ding ding ding ding ding ding' went the piano and the spotlight returned to the top of the bridge where, in a long coronation robe stood Colin, full of bonhomie, dressed as King Wolfgang.

Chapter 70

Coffee and Bailey applauded Colin's King Wolfgang, smiling at the top of the stage and waving to his subjects. Wolfgang had been their time travelling guest and they held him in great affection. They jumped up, with the rest of the tzus following suit, to see Wolfgang/Colin stood there and bearing an uncanny likeness to him with his full beard.

Wolfgang/Colin held on to the rail. He had a bad leg due to an accident in his youth, but this didn't stand in his way. He took a telescope from his pocket and looked around, as if in Scout Tower.

"I think we have some lost tzus to rescue from the water King Wolfgang?" asked Mac, taking his free paw and walking down the stairs with him, then quickly hot-pawing it up back to his narrator spot.

The stage lighting switched to a bubble filter that turned the stage in to an underwater scene representing Wolfgang Waters, where he had been lost at sea. He pretend-swam around, sat on a stool and jumped with delight when two of the ensemble appeared before him. Yet then, a look of horror as an enormous time burp appeared stage left and made towards them. He pushed the two puppies stage right and on to the staircase and, by the time the bubble had exited, the stool was empty, and the stage fell dark and silent once again.

"Wolfgang? Wolfy? Where are you?" said a shy, tearful and fearful voice from the bridge. Elegant in a flowing robe wearing silk gloves and a headscarf stood Phoebe as Queen Sally.

Chapter 71

Sally/Phoebe looked crestfallen when Wolfgang failed to return, but she smiled when Centime appeared from the shadows, playing the role of Princess Stella and holding the two puppies he had thrown to safety. To a delighted crowed the puppies acted out the scene of Wolfgang's last known movements and Sally/Phoebe smiled.

It seemed from nowhere, the time burp returned and out of it stepped Wolfgang himself! He staggered and fell into their arms.

"Time travel has exhausted him," Mac commented, "and he closes his eyes for the last time, surrounded by his friends".

As director of the show, he wanted to handle this sensitively as they all had recent memories of King Wolfgang. Quietly, Centime accompanied him off the stage and he waved a gentle goodbye. The audience sniffed and waved back. Mac had pitched it just right.

Sally/Phoebe sat on the bed, forlorn. She lowered her head as if to cry but jumped up. She ran off stage and returned with a pile of cushions and Luna the fairy. Luna waved her magic wand around and they giggled as they boinged on the bed.

"Well, we have seen a magical day here – behold the creation of the Comforter Wing! An enchanted place for all rescued tzus to recover and enchanted so the bad times fade from their memories".

Mac's words resonated with Coffee and Bailey and they smooched in on the sofa.

The stage returned to darkness.

"BELLISIMO!" bellowed an Italian accent from the bridge. King Romeo had arrived, a perfect comedy vehicle for Paddy!

Chapter 72

"Ladies and gentlefurs...try to keep calm," laughed Mac as Romeo/Paddy soaked up the attention and laughter, "it's the romantic King Romeo.....swooooooo-oooooon!"

The ensemble lined the staircase as Romeo/Paddy descended, throwing red petals and pretending to faint as the handsome King figure made his way to an adoring cast.

Paddy was loving it and building his part with every air kiss!

He waltzed around the stage with every pup, boy or girl, stopping every few minutes to brush his fur or fluff up his plume.

Everyone was in hysterics, even Mac who had, until now, stuck entirely to script.

Romeo/Paddy paused in thought and looked around the stage. He had an idea. On ran a young tzu with a watering can and he acted with it.

From the stage floor, the ensemble rose wearing flower hats, waving their leaf-covered paws.

"Yes, it was that old romantic King Romeo that planted our rose gardens," chuckled Mac.

Romeo/Paddy bowed and threw out some more kisses and petals to the audience as he backed off the stage for it to fall silent and dark again.

But not for long, it was about to get extremely noisy.

Chapter 73

"Groovy!!!"

Sammy's paws appeared from the side of the stage in heeled boots, followed by the rest of him in a tight, blue, striped single-breasted suit, white belt, red dotty shirt and flowery cravat. His floppy fur and a large pair of glasses completed the look.

"Up on your paws," Mac shouted, "dance the 'Shaggy Dog' with King Groovy!"

On the stage and amongst the audience the ensemble appeared to lead the guests in the new dance.

They jumped. They jazz-pawed. They skipped. With their hips and paws they swung to the left, they swung to the right. They wiggled their bums to each other and did the twist.

"Great shih tzus...YEAH!" bellowed Groovy/Sammy.

"Oh behave!" answered Mac.

"Let's all go again!" yelled Groovy/Sammy.

They jumped, jazz pawed, skipped, swung, wiggled and twisted again.

"Coffee and Bailey – you've got it!" Mac cheered, "...come up on to the stage!"

To the delight of the crowd, the stunned and laughing couple ascended the stage and joined the cast.

JUMP! JAZZ PAWS! SKIP! SWING! WIGGLE! TWIST!

The audience cheered again at the sight of their rulers dancing such a crazy dance. Even though they were experienced dancers, this was an amazing spectacle.

"Well done King Bailey and Queen Coffee!" Mac congratulated as Groovy/Sammy helped them to their seats and scarpered out of the back of the room.

Once again, darkness.

Chapter 74

A voice boomed across the empty stage.

"Well it's one for the money..."

"What's two for?" asked Mac.

"It's two for the show!"

"And three...?"

"Three to get ready. Now go, dog, go..."

A burst of light hit the stage to reveal King Elvis and, to everyone's delight, played by the once shy Bentz looking amazing with his top knot slicked back, blue jeans and the coolest black jacket you could ever have seen.

He strummed his guitar enthusiastically singing a 'Tzu Aroo' classic.

"But don't you
Step on my blue suede tzus
Well you can do anything
But stay off of my blue suede tzus..."

The King and Queen cheered young Elvis/Bentz with the rest of the crowd. He had proved he was a brave young lion and they were proud.

"Feel the fear and do it anyhoo!" Bailey whispered to Coffee. It was something she had taught him in their early days on the lake.

"Blue Blue...blue suede tzus..." he continued as he danced off stage right.

Chapter 75

An explosion of glitter made every fur jump and then giggle.

"Oh, my goodness," exclaimed Mac over a guitar solo, "are you ready for the 'shih tzu of the revolution'?"

A spotlight illuminated a glam-rock Percy in oversize afghan coat and flared trousers, teetering on a pair of platform boots. Gingerly, he picked his way down the stairs as King Bolan, the last of the rock star kings!

Bolan/Percy was centre stage with the whole ensemble around him letting off glitter bombs and throwing sparkling ticker tape in the air. It was everywhere and the stage sparkled and twinkled.

The ensemble swayed with him as he sang out whilst trying to stand in his platforms and not trip on his coat.

He loved it, but now it was time for the sun to set on the Rockstar era and he led the ensemble off stage, their song getting quieter as they went.

Silence descended upon a rather messy stage. It was tidy time.

Chapter 76

On the bridge Brickie arrived and gasped at the glittery mess down below with his paws clasped over his mouth. It was time to smarten things up in Tzu Kingdom after such a crazy time.

Mac passed him a hard hat and, as he ran down the stairs to where the ensemble was gathering with mops and brooms, he put on a white overall and snapped a pair of rubber gloves on to his paws.

"King Muffin likes things tidy – get ready for a clean-up!" Mac barked.

In the middle of the stage, Muffin/Brickie put his paws on his hips and shook his head.

KNOCK KNOCK

KNOCK KNOCK

The ensemble, dressed in tabards and headscarves, tapped their broom and mop handles on the floor.

KNOCK KNOCK

KNOCK KNOCK

They formed two lines and expertly threw their apparatus in the air, catching what they had swapped.

Muffin/Brickie applauded as they shimmied around him, making music with their tools as they cleaned.

Coffee smiled in the audience. They must have rehearsed long hours as not one mistake was made in any of the six throw-and-swaps.

The dance finished and the tzus-with-brooms swept up the glitter and left the stage, followed by the tzus-with-mops that finished the cleaning.

Running his paw along the clean stage, Muffin/Brickie breathed in the smell of lemon and vinegar and walked majestically off stage, leaving the Kingdom beautifully clean and smelling delightful.

"And so...the tradition of 'tidy teams' began with King Muffin..." narrator Mac told the audience, "...but it needed a little extra something doesn't you think?"

The audience wondered what it could be and their curiosity was soon solved as the ensemble dragged on beanbags in every colour of the rainbow. In the centre they whisked a large flowery beanbag around to reveal Queen Gypsophilia, played by Lola.

Chapter 77

Stunning her love Mac in her tiara of flowers, the audience gasped as Gypsophilia/Lola rose from her beanbag and floated to the stage in a gown of frills.

The ensemble, under her direction, spread cosy blankets, cushions and throws on all the seats and, within a few moments, the barren stage was an abundance of colour, comfort and warmth. The stage was starting to resemble the Tzu Kingdom they knew today, and Bailey smiled at Coffee, the one who always kept it tidy, clean and cheerful.

The lights dimmed to reveal a starry backdrop against the back curtain, and everyone sat in their beanbags and relaxed. Mac looked down, grinning from ear to ear. Then he jumped at the sound of bagpipes next to him! He had supposed to move away but Lola distracted him as Gypsophilia and he got a full blast in his ear from the bridge!

Resplendent in a green tartan kilt, it was Winny as King Hamish, playing 'Mull of Tzu Kingdom' whilst the 'Tzu Aroo' band accompanied him with a haunting drum beat and ting of a triangle.

"Is he really playing the bagpipes?" Bailey asked Coffee.

She passed her glasses to him. "He sure is, look at him puff and blow".

Bailey peered through and smiled. Winny was a special fur and no mistake, putting in all that effort as well as being a Scout and a Tzu Baker.

"What a sweet boy," he exclaimed, proudly.

As he took a bow, the audience clapped and cheered at the quiet, hardworking and popular tzu.

"Mmmmmm what is that tasty aroma?" said Mac, dreamily.

Chapter 78

The spotlight settled on a café table, set centre stage and a jewel-laden, sophisticated Kiki strode on to stage as Belgian Queen Mirabelle. She lifted the pot lid and breathed in the smell of cream, garlic and parsley - Moules Marinière.

Sitting elegantly at the bistro table she pulled her gloves off her paws finger by finger and began to sip a cocktail.

Mac narrated her scene.

"The food at Tzu Kingdom has always been good but sweet Mirabelle took it to a new level!"

Alice appeared at the door to the café and everyone gasped when they realised who she was cast as – dear sweet Nancy.

Nancy/Alice delicately tip-pawed over and joined Mirabelle/Kiki. Together they sampled dishes of food brought to them by the ensemble, dressed as waiting staff.

They giggled, laughed and danced until they flopped in to a beanbag that was then swirled around by an ensemble tzu. When it faced the audience again Nancy/Alice remained but the Queen had been replaced by a very popular King indeed. It was Pierre, from France, Bailey's predecessor, played by French resident Louis Battenberg.

Chapter 79

"Let's welcome our dear King Pierre!" Mac shouted, encouraging the audience to applaud. Many had known Pierre as ruler, and it was important to get him right. Louis was perfect casting.

Pierre was a gentle fur – kind and polite but also a whole heap of fun!

He offered his paw to Nancy/Alice who stood next to him, beckoning him down to her. She whispered something in his ear, and he gasped then nodded. She made her way to a telescope and looked out to the audience.

"The secret is told," Mac narrated, as she scoured the audience until she settled upon Coffee. "I believe Nancy has found the first of the chosen ones!" he continued as she ran over to Pierre/Louis who looked through the microscope.

"Look at those ears!" swooned Pierre/Louis to Nancy/Alice's enthusiastic nodding. They both thudded to the floor, to the amusement of Bailey and Coffee, making everyone laugh. The giggling continued as the pair arose and wandered around the stage as if concussed.

"Your ears have a lot to answer for my darling," Bailey whispered loudly to his wife, for every fur to hear. He kissed her ear and made her blush.

Back on stage, the pair were joined by two of the youngest ensemble cast members as Franc and Centime, Pierre's young brother and sister. Now it was their turn to hear the secret of the chosen one, they gasped, throwing their paws over their mouths and shook paws with Pierre.

"What an example," Mac nodded, "so young and entrusted with a big secret and they kept it too, just as promised".

"Now, who is this up here in Scout Tower?"

Looking through a telescope on the bridge was Maisie. The stage was dark again but for a lone spotlight that fixed on Stanley. Or, as they were in the show, Young Miss Coffee and Young Bailey.

Coffee/Maisie saw Bailey/Stanley in her telescope, and she cried in horror as she saw him stagger and collapse, unconscious – or worse.

"We have spied our second chosen one, but will he make it to the throne?" Mac queried as the spotlight dimmed.

The curtain fell, leaving the audience on the edge of their seats, eager to know what would happen next.

A clatter from behind made them swiftly turn around and a motor from the front made them turn back just as quickly as a screen unfurled in front of the curtain and a projector began to display a short film.

The Story of Coffee and Bailey: The Chosen Ones

Chapter 80

To the delightful sound of Luna and Tzu Aroo, the tale unfolded before the audience in a series of photos.

CLUNK CLICK

A photo of Bailey sat up in bed in the Comforter Wing, recovering from his ordeal with Coffee knelt next to him with a tray of tea and doughnuts.

CLUNK CLICK

The pair of them ready to go on a boat trip on Coffee's lake.

CLUNK CLICK

Laughing outside Tzu Bakery in their uniforms, wearing each other's hats.

CLUNK CLICK

With King Pierre and Nancy at a formal luncheon with rulers from another dog world.

CLUNK CLICK

Holding paws on stage on the day Bailey became King.

CLUNK CLICK

At the coronation of King Bailey, next to his official portrait.

CLUNK CLICK

At their wedding in Paris, in the shadow of the Eiffel Tower.

CLUNK CLICK

In the Welcome Room heading to an awards night for tzus of achievement.

CLUNK CLICK

With Paddy, Stanley, Phoebe and Maisie on the night Coffee stood down as Chief Scout and Paddy took the reins.

CLUNK CLICK

A Christmas photo with Santa Paws Shay, Embry, Binky and Pixie from Santa Paws Land.

CLUNK CLICK

With King Wolfgang and Nancy, by the waterfall.

CLUNK CLICK

A stunning photo with Tuxie, the now retired Tzu Aroo singer.

CLUNK CLICK

On their patio, enjoying a candlelit dinner.

The crowd applauded as the projector stopped and furled away, the curtains opened to the sound of Mac crooning with Luna atop the stage, where everyone joined in.

> "We'd like to teach the world to sing
> In perfect harmony
> And then to hold it in our paws
> To keep it company

"That's the song we would sing..."

> "We'd like to build the world a home
> And furnish it with love
> Grow apple trees and honey bees
> And snow-white turtle doves

"That's the song we would sing..."

"We'd like to see the world for once
All standing paw in paw
And hear them echo through the hills
For peace like Tzu Kingdom".

"That's the song we would sing..."

"Join in everyone!"

Bailey/Stanley and Coffee/Maisie walked down the stage left stairs paw-in-paw and once in the centre of the stage the entire cast began to assemble, until everyone was singing the wishful song in front of thousands of twinkling, colourful fairy lights.

"My green frock!" Coffee exclaimed. "No wonder I couldn't find it. How did it get there?"

Suddenly she was aware of Mabel and Myrtle sniggering beside her and she twigged.

"Did you two snaffle it away when we had afternoon tea in the Royal Chamber last week?"

The ladies nodded and giggled, and Coffee quickly joined in.

Around them, the audience were on their paws, singing along and they joined in too. But there were some surprises still to come...

Chapter 81

Still singing and in full costume (apart from the Chelsea Boots and platform shoes that had been kicked off backstage), Sammy and Percy ran down to the audience and, to everyone's surprise, opened the side door to the gardens.

'BEEP BEEP! BEEP BEEP!' went the Tzu Kingdom Bus as it was slowly and carefully driven in to the Party Room by Brodie with Rousey, Otis and Zeus waving from the windows. It had been beautifully liveried to celebrate the occasion, and everyone admired the painting of the royal couple on the restored bus.

Bailey laughed. At last he knew what they had wanted to restore the old bus for – and it was more than just a 'tinkering project' as he had been informed. It looked amazing and it had certainly kept them busy for a few months. He couldn't wait to take Coffee for a spin.

But it had also been a diversion. Sammy and Percy opened the other doors and as it exited the other side something amazing had arrived on stage amidst the singing cast.

The Tzu Renew cake!

* * *

"King Bailey and Queen Coffee," Mac began as the singing faded, "please join us on stage once again to celebrate the renewal of your marriage vows".

They did as they were asked, to a standing ovation, and admired the enormous cake. Jiro, Acting Chief Baker, took them through each layer from the sausages, to the pork pies and up to the cake and ice cream layers, finally pointing at the top where two tiny figures of themselves stood in the shadow of the Eiffel Tower.

"I think it's time we said a few words," said King Bailey to his wife. He whispered in her ear and she stepped forward.

Chapter 82

"Oh, my darling tzus, I just have no idea where to start saying thank you," Coffee began.

"When Bailey proposed for the, ahem, third time, I thought we would just have a nice informal service on the patio and, maybe, a sandwich spread. I could never have imagined this day if I dreamt all day! It has been truly spectacular, and we just feel so special".

"Mac, I want to thank you sweetheart for directing and narrating the show. I want to thank every single one of you that took part – from the costume and set makers, to the cast, the Tzu Bus restoration team, the catering team, everyone backstage, Tzu Aroo, Tzu Bakery...truly I don't know where to start or finish! It has just been amazing... wonderful and amazing – Bailey and I are the luckiest dogs in the world! Thank you! Thank you!"

Coffee dabbed her eyes with her handkerchief as happy tears fell. Bailey stepped forward.

"Coffee is absolutely correct – we are the luckiest dogs in the world, and I echo the thank you message. This has been the best day of my life. Not only did I get to marry this beautiful fur once again, but this time with all our friends here by our sides and we shared the history of our enchanted Kingdom. Coffee, Queen of Tzu Kingdom, I love you Sweetpea".

"Tzu Kingdom is a magical place, and without it, I would not be standing before you today and neither would many others. The only sadness in this lucky boy's heart is that every tzu is not as fortunate as we are. We do all we can here in Tzu Kingdom looking out for every less fortunate tzu we can find in the world, rescuing them, restoring their health, partying together, finding new homes for those that were unloved and sharing friendship and love. I would like to ask you all to do one thing for me".

"Uphold the traditions of Tzu Kingdom whenever you jump through the fairy doors. Do your best, be your best, look out for others and enjoy every moment here. There will be times of sadness, times of worry and there will be times of delight and times of excitement. Through all of this, face things together and hold each other's paws.

"If you do this for me and trust in the Kingdom, then we will ensure that it is, was and always will be our happy place".

The crowd, applauded, cried and cheered. Bailey smiled; he knew that promise would be kept. He looked at Coffee and winked.

The Queen asked for hush and then announced.

"I think it's time for a celebratory paw stomp!"

Chapter 83

Coffee and Bailey led everyone in the most energetic of Paw Stomps and, for the first time, Maisie was the last tzu stomping, narrowly beating Kiki and Lola. Paddy and Stanley had made it to the final twenty – a personal best thanks to their recent fitness campaign.

Sammy and the ensemble showed everyone the moves to the 'Shaggy Dog' again and it looked like this was going to be the next craze to hit the Tzu Kingdom dance floor!

The King and Queen sliced through the Tzu Renew Cake, although the ice cream layer had been popped in a Tupperware and saved in the freezer for a summer's day. They dished out plates of cake on request – the sausage, Battenberg and fruit cake layers proving to be the most popular. The cake was enormous and would be enjoyed for many weeks yet.

Exhausted from a tremendous day, the rulers announced that they were to go home but every fur was welcome to party until they could party no more. The tzus formed an arch from stage to fairy door and they ran through giggling, paw in paw, barking good night to all their friends.

At the fairy door they turned to wave and blew kisses as they jumped through to Coffee's house in Roseneath, Canada, from where Bailey would return to Essex, England, once he had seen his wife in to her home and in to her Momma's arms.

* * *

Burp. Burp.

"There my darling, home safe and sound. Is that Momma coming to the door? Oh no, it's Dad...Captain Jeff".

211

"Oh yes, dinner bell any moment now. I suspect Momma is chopping salad to go with BBQ burgers...not that I think I could eat another morsel today!" she giggled.

"Try and eat a little or they will worry you are unwell. I think it will be dinner and bed for me when I get home to Mum. I am exhausted, but happy. I honestly do think that was the best day of my life".

"Bailey Boo, I do love you to the moon my dear husband".

"I love you twice around the moon, with a waltz amongst the stars and back down to Earth my sweet Coffee".

With a kiss and a hug, Coffee ran from the cedar tree and up the steps to her house. They exchanged glances one more time and she watched as Bailey jumped through her fairy door to his home.

Chapter 84

Queen Coffee was snuggled in between her parents on the big bed when she awoke with a start as a gentle paw stroked her head.

"Bailey? Bailey Boo? What are you doing here? What time is it?"

She hastily began to comb her ears with her claws.

"Darling, your ears look beautiful, I love the silvery tones, they sparkle in the moonlight. Come with me," he held out his paw, "I have something wonderful to show you".

Confused, she wondered how he could see her ears in such detail. They had become more multi-tonal as she had grown mature, but Bailey had never noticed this since his eyesight had begun to fail.

That's when she noticed something very different about him. Angel Wings.

"What do you want to show me sweetheart?" she asked as she climbed on to his back.

Bailey's eyes twinkled as he answered, "Biscuit Mountain".

* * *

They soared high above the mountain peaks as Bailey pointed out the icing capped summits, the jam pools and the custard falls.

Wolfgang and Nancy had been here to greet him, he told her. He waved when he saw Pierre sat with Leo on a bench in a strawberry patch. Coffee couldn't see them, but she waved too, knowing that they were there for sure. The real kings and queens had gathered to welcome him here, Bailey said, just like in the show they had enjoyed the evening before.

Coffee knew that her husband's time had come, and she took comfort in the knowledge that he would be happy here, amongst tzu friends, restored to his most handsome and in the best of health.

She leaned forward and nuzzled in to his soft, warm fur for what would be the very last time until they were paw-in-paw again one day, beyond the clouds, together on Biscuit Mountain.

Chapter 85

In Tzu Kingdom, the days following King Bailey's death had been quiet. Queen Coffee had arrived in the late afternoon and sent word that she requested an audience with her senior team. Within the hour, they gathered around her in the Royal Chamber, immediately sensing that something was wrong.

Gently, with compassion, she told them that their beloved King had died in his sleep, peacefully, at home, as he would have wished.

There were tears, of course, and they held each other tight as they struggled to absorb the news.

They asked their Queen what had happened. She explained that it was simply his time to close his eyes for the last time. No one really knew how old Bailey was, but he was 15 at least, maybe older, and he had a terrible early life and it took its toll.

But he looked so well at 'Tzus Renew', they had remarked. Had it been too much for him? Was it their fault? Was it the dancing?

She bowed her head and admitted that, in recent months, Bailey's health had been declining. His sight was poor, he was often tired and he had lost a little weight but, in typical fashion, he didn't want to upset or burden anyone. As for whether the party was too much well, even if it was, it was the best day of his life, he had told her as much, so what better day to be his last.

Could they have done anything to save him, they pondered?

No, Coffee told them. It wasn't about saving him; it was simply his time to go. Like he always said, 'it is as it is, as it was and as it always will be'. They all had their time and, one day, every one of them would be on the Remember Wall in Tzu Gallery, with tzus of the future where they stood now, as they currently stood in the place their forefurs once had.

Is his human Mum ok? Myrtle the Comforter had asked, concerned as they were so bonded, as they all noticed the picture of them on his desk.

The Queen reassured them. She was devastated, much like they were but she too had noticed he was becoming frailer and was walking in to things and had been expecting his life to end. But she was strong, brave like a lion, and she wouldn't let the basket get cold. Bailey would be happy to see another dog running and playing in the home he had enjoyed. Maybe they could look out for one.

"What about you Coffee, my dear, are you OK?" asked Mabel the Comforter.

"I miss him with all my heart, but I am the best tzu I can be from having him by my side and I know he loved me. What's more, most importantly, he was loved. This will give me the strength to continue our work".

"We all loved him," said Paddy.

"What do we do now Coffee?" asked Phoebe.

"We do just what Bailey asked us to do in his final King's Speech to you all. Today, as you tell your teams and your friends that he has passed, hold paws, get through the sad times together, appreciate the happy times, find those tzus-less-fortunate and make this our happy place".

"Ask yourself in all you do – what would King Bailey do?"

Chapter 86

Queen Coffee stood looking out of the patio doors at the swing where she had enjoyed many romantic evenings with Bailey. Her heart ached as she held a framed photograph of them together in their youth on her boat.

She stroked his face and a tear fell on his image but, this time, he didn't come back to life. He remained there, with that twinkle in his eyes yet frozen in time. Young Bailey with Young Coffee on a day trip with her Momma and Dad, long before they ascended to their thrones.

A knock at the door startled her, but with the smell of lemon and vinegar wafting in from the paws of the Chief Scout and Deputy Scout after finishing their shift and cleaning Scout Tower, she knew just who it was.

"Can we come in?" asked Paddy, even though he was in, with Stanley, and the door was already closing behind them.

"We made you this...a sweet pea basket, because we know that was Bailey's pet name for you. Well, Sweetpea, not basket..."

Coffee giggled as Stanley blushed and Paddy poked him in the tummy.

"Thank you boys. What a thoughtful gift. I shall put this on the patio to enjoy. It smells delicious, what good tzus you are".

"We thought you might like us to accompany you to the Party Room for the Royal Announcement, as it's the first one you have done...erm...alone," offered Paddy.

As she took the basket through to the patio, they followed her with their eyes and Stanley saw something that troubled him.

"Queen Coffee, why are all your and King Bailey's photographs in a box?"

"Oh dear, you weren't supposed to see this," Coffee chewed her paws, "you two had best sit down".

They did, at some speed.

"Well, as you know Bailey's health had been deteriorating and I'm not getting any younger so, a few months ago we made a decision – to retire together".

The boys' eyes were like saucers, they were shocked. It was like the bottom had fallen out of their world.

"But things have changed now," Stanley hoped, "you won't retire as Queen, will you?"

She lowered her eyes and nodded.

"Yes, we had talked it through and decided we would follow the example of Santa Paws. They serve for a maximum of seven years – twenty-one dog years – and then they become the 'Santa Paws Emeritus' as Shay will be before too long. It allows for a paw-over and we felt that was the right thing for us too. Bailey wished to return to Tzu Bakery to continue his quest for the perfect doughnut and I was to become a comforter. Goodness knows, they need help down there. Plus, we wanted to spend some quality time together".

"...and now?" Paddy ventured.

"That's what my announcement is Paddy, I am going to be 'Queen Coffee Emeritus, Comforter'. Tzu Kingdom will seek a new ruler. It's time for a fresh chapter".

Stanley sobbed and Paddy consoled him.

"Darling boys, I only became Queen to support my Bailey Boo and I have no appetite to serve alone. The story of Coffee and Bailey is at an end, it's time".

"Can I tell you two a secret, something no one else knows?"

They nodded. Coffee took a deep breath to tell them how it all began, with a secret that not even Nancy had known.

"Every day, every second of Bailey's life was a beautiful bonus. When I found him that day in the forest, he was dead. I cried and my enchanted tears landed on his fur and brought him back to life. From those fragile beginnings he became the most wonderful King and, if the legend is true, the chosen one".

"So, I protected him and treasured him every day. We were, again if the legend of the 'chosen ones' is true, how Tzu Kingdom became what it is today through time burps and magic – 'as it is, as it was and as it always will be'.

"I think this is why I am ready to start a new phase in my life, our time was amazing, incredible, special and unforgettable. Now the path is paved for the future of Tzu Kingdom. Every one of us is who we are because we had Bailey in our lives and he will always be with us".

She paused. Not sure whether to tell them another secret but concluding that they would always keep her confidence.

"I saw him once more you know. He appeared to me as an angel. I don't know if it really happened or whether it was a dream, I had the same about Nancy, but he had resplendent wings and flew me to a place called Biscuit Mountain..."

Stanley coughed and spluttered. Paddy gasped.

"Tell her Stan...you've got to!"

She spun around. "Stanley?"

"Queen Coffee, when I was upset at Christmas and I ran away well, I had a visitor from Biscuit Mountain. I have only told Pads but, well, King Wolfgang came to me when I was troubled. He helped me understand some stuff but, well, he told me about it. He said they were happy, together and restored to their most glorious. He too had resplendent angel wings!"

"Then it's true," Coffee smiled as she flopped on a beanbag next to them, "because when he came to me, he could see my ears properly again and remarked on their silvery tones".

"That means that he's happy, relaxed and at his most handsome once again, his eyes work perfectly once more, and he can keep watch over us all".

They hugged each other and before they knew it were doing the 'Shaggy Dog' and shimmying, just like Bailey would do.

Chapter 87

They prepared to leave for the announcement in a sad but happy mood.

"Can I still call you QC when you retire?" Paddy asked.

"Of course, you can," she assured him.

"Boys, I am going to announce my retirement and then I am going to go away for a few days so the election can begin for the new ruler. Santa Paws Shay, Pixie, Binky and Embry had invited us to stay for a long weekend. Shay wrote with his condolences and pleaded with me to keep to our plans and I said yes".

"A rest will do you good," Stanley nodded, sagely.

"I wonder who our next ruler will be?" Paddy puzzled.

"Well, any tzu can stand, it only takes the nomination of one other. I hope you two will be putting yourselves forward," the retiring Queen replied.

"US?" they declared, as one, laughing hysterically and slapping each other on their backs. But Coffee wasn't laughing.

"I'm serious," she said, "you two are strong contenders. Along with Phoebe, Tanner, Mac, Alice, Centime, Franc...new furs such as Bentz and Winny, Maisie, Michelle...there's a long list of qualified tzus...Lola, Kiki, Lennon. Any one of you could be the next King or Queen of Tzu Kingdom".

The boys were aghast. Coffee laughed again.

"Just ask yourself WWKBD?"

They looked perplexed.

"What Would King Bailey Do?"

* * *

Paddy and Stanley opened the doors to the Party Room, full of tzus once again, awaiting their Queen.

Coffee walked to the stage and thanked them for their escort and ascended to address the kingdom.

"Tzus, I have an important announcement to make..." her lip began to quiver, and she covered her face with her paw.

In the audience, Maisie nudged Beth. "She needs a paw to hold, come on, Nancy would have been with her and we are her sisters".

The two girls ran up and took a paw each, giving her the strength to carry on and she began her speech with courage and confidence.

Paddy put his paw around Stanley, who hugged him close.

"Brave as a lion time..." said Stanley.

BOOK 4: THE JEWEL EYE CROWN

To be released Summer 2020

the final book in the series...

Visit www.tzukingdom.com

for release updates, news and short stories

Find 'Tzu Kingdom' on Facebook, Twitter and
Instagram

See www.toonpetz.com to have your pet illustrated
in the Tzu Kingdom style.

Read the true story of Bailey's rescue on
www.tzukingdom.com/bailey.html

About the Authors

Karen Chilvers was born in Essex in 1971 and lives in Brentwood with her dogs and cats including King Bailey. She much prefers Tzu Kingdom to the real world and has a fairy themed garden.

Gill Eastgate was born in Edinburgh in 1971. As a child she wanted a pony but ended up with a rabbit. Stanley is her first dog who has, quite simply, changed her life. She lives in a suburb of Edinburgh with Stan and her husband Ray, who is affectionately known as 'The Tzu Father' due to his tzu-inspired beard.

Karen and Gill met in 2013 through Bailey and Stan after they both joined Twitter and introduced their mums to each other, knowing they had a lot in common. They first met in person in 2015, when Karen rocked up to Edinburgh for the festival and ensconced herself in Gill's house for three days. Stan slept on her bed and it was during that trip that the first part of the Tzu Kingdom series was scribed.

Many of the dogs in Tzu Kingdom are based on real dogs throughout the world that met on twitter forming firm and lasting friendships.

Acknowledgements

Karen would like to thank her mum for being there always, her sister Claire for giving her someone to have a wild imagination for in her youth, her nephew Freddie for allowing her to bring that back to life but, most of all Bailey, her inspiration. Book 3 is largely based on his true rescue that saw him go from unwanted, unloved and close-to-death stray to international sensation King Bailey of Tzu Kingdom. A special and enduring bond.

Gill would like to thank the wonderful world of Twitter, after all, without it Karen and Gill would never have met. Her mum just for being her mum, her husband Ray for listening intently to the happenings in Tzu Kingdom without thinking she was completely mad, her wonderful Shih Tzu Stanley and, of course, her much loved and sadly missed Dad.

Karen and Gill both wish to thank actor Callum Hughes for voicing Stanley in the short film 'Stanley's Secret', Michelle Smith and ToonPetz.com for the beautiful illustrations that have also raised funds for furs-less-fortunate and all their fur-friends across the world that have equipped a bus, supported us and made us laugh and cry over the years.

We love you to the moon.

Printed in July 2019
by Rotomail Italia S.p.A., Vignate (MI) - Italy